JOURNEY TO CRYSTAL MOUNTAIN BOOK 3

A MIDDLE GRADE LITRPG FANTASY ADVENTURE

THE CRYSTAL MOUNTAIN SAGA
BOOK 3

TIMOTHY MCGOWEN

ILLUSTRATED BY
CANDACE MORRIS

EDITED BY
CANDACE MORRIS

BIBLIOGRAPHY OF TIMOTHY MCGOWEN

HAVEN CHRONICLES

Haven Chronicles: Eldritch Knight

THE CRYSTAL MOUNTAIN SAGA

Journey To Crystal Mountain Book 1
Journey To Crystal Mountain Book 2
Journey To Crystal Mountain Book 3

LAST BORN OF KI'DARTH

Reincarnation: A Litrpg/Gamelit Trilogy
Rebellion: A Litrpg/Gamelit Trilogy
Retribution: A Litrpg/Gamelit Trilogy

ORDER & CHAOS

Arcane Knight Book 1: An Epic LITRPG Fantasy
Arcane Knight Book 2: An Epic LITRPG Fantasy
Arcane Knight Book 3: An Epic LITRPG Fantasy
Arcane Knight Book 4: An Epic LITRPG Fantasy
Arcane Knight Book 5: An Epic LITRPG Fantasy

THE ELEMENTAL REALMS

Nexus Guardian Book 1: A Fantasy LitRPG Adventure
Nexus Guardian Book 2: A Fantasy LitRPG Adventure

REVIEWS ARE IMPORTANT

Every review matters, get your voice heard.

Follow me on Amazon to get informed when my next book is released!

https://www.amazon.com/stores/Timothy-McGowen/author/B087QTTRJK

Join my Patreon for early Chapters!

https://www.patreon.com/TimothyMcGowen

Join my Facebook group and discuss the books

https://www.facebook.com/groups/234653175151521/

SPECIAL THANKS

I wanted to give a special thanks to those that helped bring this book to its current state.

Candace Morris - Alpha Reader, Beta Reader, Editor, and Proofer

Thank you.

*I dedicate this book to all my nieces and nephews, good luck
on the adventures of life.*

CONTENTS

SUMMARY

Book 2 Summary:

What an adventure it has been! We went from dinosaurs on the beach and jungle to bugs in a cave looking to take us out, but we've learned so much. Zack got separated from the team, learned some hard lessons, and was reunited with his team toward the end of the book. The group traveled into a cave to seek out the elemental stone, and after much fighting and hard work, they found it! Now they have one part left in their journey, return the Elemental Stone to the Crystal Mountain! Can they do it and what dangers lie ahead? They've learned to work together and nothing will stand in their way!

CHAPTER 1
ZACK - PREPARATIONS

They really believed in me as their leader, and that made me proud to take on the role. At first I'd wanted to be the leader because it sounded so cool, but now, I'd learned that being a leader meant listening to those you were meant to lead. It also helped to not want to be a leader, a mind set shift that allowed one to become a better leader, assuming they were up to the task. And I truly felt like I could do it, but a part of me still wondered if I was the right pick.

Addy walked ahead toward our beach front base and I couldn't help but admire her from afar. Really she ought to be our leader, but she'd chosen me instead and I'd do my best to fill that position and be worthy of her trust. She was so strong, confident, and well pretty cute as well. She seemed to sense my eyes on her and she turned to look at me, smiling in my direction.

The walk to the base took only a few minutes, the area we'd been let out of was a cave like place on the beach and it seemed to close itself behind us after we left, almost as if it knew we were passing through it. That was an odd feeling to have, but I took it in stride, because this island was a place where I'd learned to expect anything at all.

The sun was out in full force and despite the cool breeze off the ocean waters, I was warm thanks to my enchanted armor, sun or not. That was good too, because if I was remembering right, mountains could be cold and we'd need to be ready for possible harsh environments on our way to return the elemental stone.

"You never gave us the whole story, how was it when you were separated from us?" Jayden asked, adjusting his glasses as his Raptor Charles walked beside him, looking more dragon like than ever before with the streaks of red and his ability to belch fire.

"It was a bit scary," I admitted, Jayden was my closest friend and it helped to be able to share things with him. Normally I'd keep it all inside, but I was trying out some new things, figuring I could trust him with my fears.

"We were super worried for you," Jayden said, then his expression went from stern to soft. "But we are glad you made your way back to us. You really have the potential to be a good leader, if you can just keep learning to listen and do what is good for the entire group."

"I'll try my best," I said, pushing away the feelings I'd

normally get when someone questioned me. I could learn to be better, I would be better, I decided.

"Thanks again for the armor," Jayden said. "I wonder if we will be able to keep anything we've made or the new friends we have."

"Wouldn't it be cool if Charles came back with us?" I asked, laughing at the prospect of a raptor showing up in school or wherever we would return to when the time came.

"I'm afraid the magical creatures, our mechanical pets, and the dinosaurs are probably meant to stay here on this island," Jayden said with confidence that surprised me. He had grown so much in such a short period of time, speaking with confidence and carrying himself in a way that spoke of the same.

"You think our families miss us yet, I feel like we've been gone forever," I said, casting my eyes down as we walked and I let my thoughts turn to my family and how I missed them, especially my mom. I was tired of disappointing her and I made an oath to myself, here and now, that I'd do better.

"I'm not sure," Jayden said, surprising me with his answer. "I don't yet know if the temporal time flow is the same there as it is here. For all we know only seconds will have passed, but I could be wrong."

"Wouldn't that be something," I said, grinning. "If we just showed up like no time had passed at all. Then we could give Mr. Shadow a piece of our mind."

W reached the beach fort and began our preparations for the journey ahead. It included collecting berries, cooking up some Dodo meat, and crafting armor and weapons for everyone. We worked as a cohesive unit, each of us doing what needed to be done to get us to the point where we could move onward.

CHAPTER 2
ADDY – THROUGH THE JUNGLE

I pushed a thick curtain of vines aside and squinted as the midday sun barely pierced through the dense canopy overhead. The jungle was alive with noise—chirping birds, rustling leaves, and the occasional distant roar of something way too big to be ignored.

"Watch your step," I warned, holding out my arm to stop Sofia before she walked straight into a tangle of thorny, vine-covered roots.

Sofia huffed, adjusting her backpack. "This island has something against clear paths, I swear."

"Wouldn't be an adventure if it was easy," Zack said, flashing one of his usual grins, though I could tell he was keeping an eye on everything around us. He was taking this leadership thing seriously, which was honestly kind of nice.

Jayden, ever the careful one, crouched and inspected

the twisted roots. "These aren't just random jungle vines," he muttered, adjusting his glasses. "They look... grown with purpose."

I frowned. "You think something planted them here?"

Before he could answer, Charles let out a deep, growling huff, his nostrils flaring. That wasn't a good sign. At all.

"Uh, guys?" Zack's voice lost a little of its confidence. "I think we're being watched."

I followed his gaze up into the tangled branches, and my stomach dropped.

Glowing yellow eyes. More than one pair. Maybe a dozen. Blinking between the branches, shifting, watching.

Sofia let out a sharp gasp. "Tell me those are fireflies and not giant tree monsters."

A deep, low chittering sound filled the air, like dry leaves rubbing together, but coming from every direction.

I gripped my Soul Band, channeling energy through it. A soft, golden glow flickered to life around my hand. "We should—"

The trees moved.

Nope. Nope, nope, nope. The trees were alive.

Long, vine-like arms unfurled from the branches, dropping down with a slow, deliberate motion. I counted three, maybe four creatures—each twisting together from bark and leaves, their faces carved into gaping wooden grins.

Sofia took one look at them and immediately backed

up. "Okay, I change my vote. This jungle officially hates us."

Zack pulled his sword free. "We can take 'em, right?"

Jayden, still analyzing, held out a hand. "Wait—don't attack yet." He was locked in that thinking mode of his, the one where he tried to figure out how to solve problems without fighting.

I shifted my stance, raising my hand. No way was I waiting for them to grab us first.

I sent a spear of light directly at the nearest tree-thing's chest. The glowing weapon slammed into it, splintering bark and sending it staggering back—but instead of retreating, the creature absorbed the glow.

My stomach twisted. "Uh. That's new."

Jayden's eyes widened. "I think they're feeding off your energy!"

Sofia groaned. "Oh, of course they are."

One of the creatures lunged for Zack, its vine-like fingers stretching toward him, but Charles was faster. The raptor leapt, jaws snapping, tearing through bark and vines like they were paper. The thing screeched and fell back, writhing.

"Fire works!" Jayden called out. "Zack—use your sword!"

Zack didn't hesitate. He swung, and his copper blade —still faintly glowing from the enchantment—cut straight through the second creature's arm. A sizzling sound filled the air.

"Elemental magic counters them!" Jayden realized.

I gritted my teeth. If light magic didn't work, then maybe...

I focused on my Soul Band, pushing for something new. My energy shifted, turning red-hot. A new spear of flame burst to life in my hand, flickering and wild.

"Let's see how they like this," I muttered.

I threw the fire spear directly into the largest of the tree creatures. The instant it made contact, the thing burst into flames, screeching as it collapsed. The fire spread, flickering up its limbs until it was nothing but cinders.

"Fire works really well!" I called.

Zack and Jayden tore through the rest, Charles finishing off the last with another burst of flame. Within minutes, the jungle was quiet again.

We stood, breathing hard, surrounded by scattered ash and smoking vines.

Sofia brushed herself off, glancing warily around. "So. That happened."

Zack grinned. "And we totally owned those things!"

I wasn't smiling yet. My mind was spinning. Those creatures absorbed my normal attacks. What if there were more enemies like that? Enemies that could counter our abilities?

I glanced toward the distant mountains through a break in the canopy.

This wasn't going to get easier.

It was going to get a whole lot harder.

CHAPTER 3
ZACK – THE RIVER'S SECRET

I wiped sweat off my forehead and squinted through the trees. The jungle had finally thinned out, and now, stretching before us, was a wide, fast-moving river. It cut through the jungle like a silver ribbon, its surface rippling under the sunlight. But something about it felt... off.

"Wait a sec," I said, frowning. "Shouldn't the water be flowing *toward* the ocean?"

Jayden crouched by the edge, adjusting his glasses as he studied the current. "Yeah. Rivers normally flow downhill, toward the lowest point... but this one is going *uphill.*"

I blinked. "That's—uh—not how water works."

Sofia knelt beside him, running a hand through the water. "It's cold. Like... way colder than it should be."

Addy tilted her head, staring down the river's length. "You think it leads to the Crystal Mountain?"

Jayden stood, his expression thoughtful. "If it's defying normal physics, then *maybe*. Magic might be keeping it flowing toward something important."

Magic. Right. I still wasn't totally used to that idea, even after all the weird, impossible things we'd seen so far.

I cracked my knuckles. "Well, if the river is heading where we need to go... why not ride it?"

Sofia groaned. "Please don't say what I think you're about to say."

"We build a raft!" I said, grinning.

Addy sighed. "Of course he said it."

Jayden actually looked interested. "That... might not be the worst idea. Traveling by river could be *faster* than cutting through more jungle. Plus, we won't have to deal with tree monsters again."

"Right?" I said, pointing at Jayden like he'd just solved an impossible equation. "See? Smart guy approves. Let's build a raft."

Sofia crossed her arms. "Assuming we don't drown in the process."

"I can make it sturdy," I said, patting my Soul Band. "Leave it to me."

We got to work, chopping down smaller trees with my copper axe and dragging over fallen logs. I let my Creation Matrix guide me, channeling magic into the wood, fusing pieces together, reinforcing the base with vines and thick branches.

By the time we were done, our raft wasn't just a pile of logs tied together—it was solid. A flat wooden deck, lashed with vine rope, with side rails to keep us from falling off.

I even added a simple rudder so we could steer.

"Whoa," Addy said, running a hand over the smooth surface. "Okay, I *wasn't* expecting it to actually look this... professional."

I grinned, setting down my axe. "I told you. I got this."

"Impressive work," Jayden admitted, checking the knots.

Sofia flicked a piece of dirt off her sleeve. "Fine. But if this thing falls apart halfway down the river, I'm blaming you."

"Noted," I said, rolling my eyes.

We pushed the raft into the water, and it actually floated perfectly.

We all climbed on—me at the front, Addy and Jayden in the middle, and Sofia gripping the side rails like she expected certain death. Charles took the back, looking entirely too comfortable for a fire-breathing dinosaur on a homemade raft.

Then... we drifted off.

The jungle slid past as the river pulled us forward. The weirdest part? It wasn't even fast-moving whitewater. It was smooth, controlled, like it wanted us to follow it.

Jayden kept studying the water, his eyebrows scrunched in concentration. "This is unnatural. It's almost like the current is... *guiding us.*"

"Good, that means less paddling," I said, resting my arms behind my head.

Then we saw the ruins.

A crumbling stone archway rose on the left bank, half-swallowed by vines and moss. Behind it, ancient pillars stretched into the trees, their surfaces covered in faded carvings.

Jayden's jaw dropped. "No way... This is evidence of an ancient civilization!"

Addy narrowed her eyes. "This island wasn't supposed to have people. Right?"

Sofia hugged herself. "Then who built that?"

I grabbed the rudder, steering the raft toward shore. "Only one way to find out."

We jumped off, splashing into the shallows. The ground sank under our feet, thick with mud and damp leaves.

Jayden practically vibrated with excitement. "Look at this! These carvings... they're telling a story."

I stepped closer, brushing dirt away from one of the engraved stone slabs. There were figures, some human-like, others monstrous, surrounding a glowing object that looked a lot like the Elemental Stone.

Addy pointed at the top section. "That looks like a mountain. See how the light rises toward it?"

Jayden nodded. "It's showing the Crystal Mountain. And look—here," he pointed at a line of figures, kneeling toward the stone. "This civilization must have worshiped the Elemental Stone. Maybe they used it to maintain balance on the island."

"Or control it," Sofia muttered.

I didn't like the way she said that.

"Guys..." I started, feeling a sudden chill crawl up my spine.

Something was off.

The air felt heavier here, like the jungle was watching us.

Then, the carvings shifted.

No. That wasn't possible. They moved.

Jayden sucked in a breath. "Did you see that?"

I did.

The stone rippled, like water.

Then, from the darkness of the ruins, a deep, echoing voice whispered—

"Return the Stone... before it is too late."

CHAPTER 4
ADDY – NIGHT UNDER THE STARS

The second I saw the carvings move, I froze.

That wasn't possible.

Stone didn't just ripple like water and whisper warnings in spooky, echoing voices.

I swallowed hard, gripping my spear of light as a cold chill ran up my spine. "Did... did that thing just talk?"

Jayden's mouth opened and closed, but no words came out.

Sofia stepped back, shaking her head. "Nope. No, thank you. We are *not* doing haunted ruins today."

Zack, because of course he would, stepped closer. "Uh, hello? Mysterious ancient voice?" He knocked on the stone. "Mind elaborating on the whole *before it's too late* thing?"

Nothing. Just silence.

I let out a slow breath, trying to calm the racing of my

heart. I felt Cappy, my little robotic monkey, squeeze onto my shoulder a bit tighter, sending a wave of warmth through me. It was his way of reassuring me, soothing my fear before it could spiral.

I reached up and gave him a small scratch behind the ears. "Okay. We're all tired, we've had a long day. Maybe we imagined it."

Jayden visibly bristled. "We didn't *imagine* anything. There's something *deeply magical* about this place. I think these ruins were left behind as a message—maybe a warning."

"Right," Sofia muttered, crossing her arms. "Because those always end *so* well."

I ignored her and stepped forward, running my hand over the carvings. Now that I was looking closer, I noticed something strange. The figures around the Elemental Stone weren't just worshiping it—some looked like they were fighting over it.

A bad feeling twisted in my gut.

Cappy made a soft chittering sound, like he knew I was overthinking again, and nuzzled against my cheek. A slow breath escaped me, and I focused on the present.

"Let's get out of here," I said, turning to Zack. "We should make camp by the river and figure things out in the morning. I don't trust this place at night."

For once, no one argued.

By the time we made it back to the raft, the sky had turned a deep shade of indigo, the first stars beginning to poke through the jungle canopy. The river was calm and quiet, the distant hum of crickets filling the air.

Zack worked on getting a fire started, Jayden helped gather driftwood, and Sofia—shockingly—helped set up a makeshift shelter using big palm leaves and the tarp she pulled from her inventory.

Cappy climbed down from my shoulder, scampering around the campsite, inspecting everything like he was making sure it was safe. The moment he finished, he hopped back onto my shoulder and sent me a feeling of reassurance.

I sat on a fallen log, watching the flames crackle and flicker. For the first time all day, things felt... peaceful.

Zack plopped down next to me, stretching out. "See? Look at us. Surviving. Thriving. Figuring out ancient mysteries."

I gave him a sideways glance. "You mean running away from haunted rock walls and building a campsite like exhausted kids lost in the woods?"

"That too," Zack admitted, grinning.

Jayden and Sofia sat across from us, Charles curled up nearby, his tail flicking lazily. Every now and then, Jayden would reach over and rub the raptor's head, and I could see the way Charles purred in response. It was weirdly comforting, seeing how much Charles grounded him.

"Alright," Zack said, rubbing his hands together. "Since we actually have *a second* to breathe, I vote we do something fun."

I raised an eyebrow. "Fun?"

"Yeah. You know, like telling stories."

Jayden perked up. "That's actually an *excellent* bonding exercise."

Sofia groaned. "Why do I feel like this is going to be embarrassing?"

Zack ignored her and grinned. "Okay, okay—who's got the best home story? You know, something about life before *all this*." He waved around dramatically.

I hesitated. Home felt... *far away*. But maybe that was why we needed this.

Jayden adjusted his glasses. "I'll go first." He cleared his throat. "When I was eight, I *accidentally* hacked into my dad's friends company server trying to figure out where he hid my Christmas presents."

Sofia snorted. "No way."

Jayden nodded seriously. "Oh, yes. I was *very* curious. But instead of finding a gift list, I triggered some kind of security lockdown and my dad's friend had to explain to his entire IT team that no, they were not being cyber-attacked, it was just his son looking for Legos."

Zack clutched his stomach laughing. "Dude. You *would* accidentally hack a company. That is *so* on brand for you."

Jayden shrugged. "It was an important learning experience."

Zack wiped his eyes. "Alright, Sofia. Your turn."

Sofia rolled her eyes. "Fine. This *one time*, I convinced

my parents I had food poisoning just so I wouldn't have to go to a violin recital."

Jayden tilted his head. "Wait. I thought you liked violin?"

Sofia smirked. "Oh, I do. I just *hated* the teacher. She was this old, mean lady who smelled like cough drops and always made me play boring songs. I wanted to play something cool, like *Pirates of the Caribbean*, not—" she dramatically wiggled her fingers, "—*Beethoven's Slowest Symphony of All Time.*"

Zack clapped. "Respect. That is some next-level strategy."

Sofia smirked, clearly pleased with herself.

Then they both looked at me.

"Alright, Addy. You're up," Zack said.

I hesitated, poking at the fire with a stick. "I... don't know if mine's that interesting."

Cappy squeaked at me, nudging against my shoulder. He wanted me to share something.

I sighed, but smiled. "Well... I did *used to help out* at my parents' clinic."

Jayden's eyes lit up. "Really?"

I nodded. "Yeah. Mostly small things. Bandaging kids, helping with check-ups. But once..." I looked up, meeting their eyes, "I got to help deliver a baby goat."

Sofia blinked. "Excuse me, *what?*"

Zack gasped dramatically. "Addy, you *midwifed* a baby goat and didn't tell us?"

I laughed. "It wasn't *that* big of a deal!"

Jayden looked genuinely impressed. "Actually, that's pretty amazing."

Zack leaned in. "Awesome?"

I nodded. "Yeah. It was *awesome.*"

A comfortable silence settled over us, the fire crackling softly. For the first time in a while, I felt normal.

Zack stretched. "Welp. That was nice. Now, let's talk fears."

Sofia groaned. "Ugh. Of course."

Cappy squeezed my hand, already soothing my nerves. I knew this was important.

One by one, we shared.

Jayden was afraid of not being useful.

Sofia was afraid of losing control.

I was afraid of failing.

Zack bumped his shoulder into mine. "Dude. Same."

I smiled, watching the stars overhead. We were scared. But together, we'd make it.

Tomorrow, the journey continued.

But tonight?

Tonight, we had each other.

CHAPTER 5
ZACK – THE SWAMP
OF ILLUSIONS

The morning started off fine. Better than fine, actually. We had full bellies, the sun was shining, and the river was carrying us straight toward Crystal Mountain. For once, everything was going smoothly.

Which, in hindsight, should have been my first clue that something was about to go *really, really wrong*.

I sat at the back of the raft, my legs stretched out in front of me, my hand idly stroking Ash's metal feathers. He leaned into me, his little mechanical claws gripping my shoulder, his presence as reassuring as ever.

Jayden studied the map, muttering about the unnatural flow of the river. "It still doesn't make sense," he said, adjusting his glasses. "We're going against gravity. There's no source high enough to be feeding this water, not at this volume."

Sofia, who was lounging on the raft with her arms

crossed behind her head, cracked an eye open. "You're still questioning how this island works?"

Jayden frowned. "I'm just saying—"

"Magic," I interrupted, waving a hand. "The answer is magic. Just like everything else that doesn't make sense around here."

Addy, standing near the front, frowned at me. "Just because we don't understand something doesn't mean we shouldn't try."

"Sure, sure," I said, leaning back. "You keep trying to figure out the mysteries of the universe, and I'll just—"

Then the river changed.

The current that had been guiding us vanished.

The raft slowed to a stop, the water beneath us turning dark and murky. Fog rolled in, thick and heavy, clinging to my skin like cold fingers. The trees on either side of the river grew twisted, their roots curling into the water like skeletal hands.

Ash let out a low *"squawk"* and shifted on my shoulder.

I swallowed. "Uh, guys?"

Addy tensed, her spear appearing in her hand in a flash of golden light. "Yeah. I feel it too."

Sofia sat up fast. "Okay, this feels *very* haunted."

Jayden glanced around, gripping his club. "There's nothing on the map about a swamp."

"Because it wasn't here before," Sofia muttered.

A chill ran down my spine.

Then I saw it.

A shadow, flickering in the mist.

A voice—soft, familiar—drifted through the fog.

"Zack..."

My stomach dropped.

I knew that voice.

I would always know that voice.

I turned slowly, my chest tightening.

Through the mist, standing on the water, was my dad.

He was exactly how I remembered him—the same scruffy beard, the same worn-out flannel shirt, the same warm, tired smile.

My legs felt weak. My breath hitched.

"You're here," he said, his voice full of something I desperately wanted to believe was real.

My throat tightened. "Dad?"

"Come here, kiddo," he said, holding out his arms like he used to when I was little. "I've missed you."

Everything else faded. The swamp. The raft. My friends.

I took a step forward.

Ash shrieked.

Then pain—sharp and hot—flared across my shoulder as Ash's metal claws dug into my skin.

The illusion shattered.

My dad's figure glitched, flickering between shapes, his face twisting, stretching—until it wasn't him at all.

I stumbled back, my breath ragged, my entire body shaking.

It wasn't real.

It was never real.

Then Jayden screamed.

I spun, my heart slamming against my ribs.

Jayden was backing up fast, his face pale, eyes wide. His lips trembled as he whispered, "No... no, you're not here... you're not here."

Charles growled, stepping in front of him, but Jayden wasn't seeing *us*. He was seeing something else.

Neil leapt onto his chest, pressing its forehead to Jayden's.

Jayden sucked in a breath—then snapped back to reality.

Sofia let out a choked sob. I turned to her just in time to see her whole body lock up.

Her eyes locked onto something past us.

Her face went pale.

She whispered, "Go away."

Her snake coiled around her arm, squeezing just enough to break her out of the illusion. She gasped, blinking rapidly, and just like that—she was free.

I clenched my fists, breathing hard.

This wasn't just illusions. This was something worse.

I didn't realize I was shaking until I felt Ash nuzzle against my cheek, his little metal wings pressing into me, his warmth spreading through my body.

And just like that—

The fear disappeared.

I snapped back.

I saw Addy, standing strong, her eyes burning with determination.

She summoned a wave of golden light and blasted it outward.

The fog ripped apart.

The illusions shattered.

And suddenly, we weren't alone.

Dozens of red eyes blinked to life in the darkness of the trees.

And then—they moved.

"Paddle!" I shouted.

Jayden and Addy grabbed the poles, pushing hard, while Sofia and I stood ready, weapons drawn.

Branches rustled. The creatures leapt.

And just like that—

We were fighting for our lives.

The first one hit the raft hard.

It was fast—faster than I expected. A shadowy blur with glowing red eyes, leaping straight from the trees.

I barely had time to react before its clawed hands slammed onto the raft, its weight tilting the whole thing sideways.

Sofia screamed.

I lunged, swinging my sword on instinct. The blade connected with something solid—a wet, crunching sound followed—and the creature howled.

It reeled back, disappearing into the mist.

Then the others came.

Dozens of them.

They dropped from the trees, clawed hands grasping, moving like they weren't fully solid—like the mist itself was part of them.

Addy shot a beam of light across the water, illuminating their twisted, shifting bodies.

They weren't human. They weren't animals.

They were something else.

"Zack, left!" Jayden shouted.

I twisted just as another one lunged.

I swung my sword, aiming low. The thing dodged midair, bending in a way that shouldn't have been possible.

It landed on the raft right in front of me.

Too close. Too fast.

Then Ash screeched.

A blur of metal wings—then impact.

Ash slammed into the thing's head, knocking it back just enough for me to react.

I kicked out, hard. The creature tumbled off the raft, screeching as it splashed into the river.

"Everyone hold on!" Addy shouted.

I barely had time to register what she meant before she slammed her spear into the water.

A shockwave of light exploded outward.

The mist ripped apart. The creatures screamed, their bodies twisting and flickering—then they vanished, dissolving into the darkness like smoke in the wind.

And just like that—the attack was over.

Silence.

The mist cleared. The glowing red eyes were gone.

We drifted.

No one spoke. No one moved.

The river carried us forward, slowly, steadily.

I swallowed hard, trying to get my breathing under control. My heart still pounded against my ribs. My hands shook, my sword felt too heavy in my grip.

Jayden was sitting down, hugging his arms to his chest, his fox curled up against him, radiating warmth. Sofia wiped at her face with trembling hands, her snake coiled tight around her arm.

Addy stood at the front of the raft, her back straight, her spear still glowing faintly in her grip.

She turned, meeting my eyes. "You okay?"

I forced a shaky breath. "Yeah."

I wasn't sure if it was true.

But I wanted it to be.

She nodded, then glanced ahead.

I followed her gaze.

The mist had finally thinned.

Ahead of us, the river opened into a wide grove, the trees parting to reveal solid ground.

A place to rest. A place to regroup.

After everything we'd just been through, I wasn't about to question it.

We had survived.

For now.

CHAPTER 6
ADDY - THE LOST VILLAGE

The raft drifted slowly into the clearing, the river widening as it reached a shallow bank. The mist still clung to the air, but it wasn't the thick, suffocating fog from before—it was lighter now, almost like a whisper against the trees.

I was the first to step off, my boots sinking slightly into the soft, mossy ground. My legs still felt unsteady after the battle, but I forced myself to stand tall.

Zack followed, gripping his sword like he expected something to jump out at us. His eyes kept darting around, scanning the treeline. On edge. I couldn't blame him.

Jayden and Sofia moved slower, exhaustion written all over their faces. Sofia's snake was still wrapped tightly around her wrist, and Neil, Jayden's fox, curled at his feet, tail twitching nervously.

Even our mechanical companions were wary.

And then—I saw it.

The village.

Hidden among the trees, past the thick roots and fallen logs, stood a cluster of old wooden huts. Some had caved-in roofs, others were swallowed by vines. A few stone pathways poked out from the overgrowth, barely visible under layers of mud and moss.

It was abandoned.

Long abandoned.

"This place looks ancient," Jayden whispered, adjusting his glasses as he took it all in.

Sofia wrinkled her nose. "It also smells like mold and regret."

Zack ignored her and took a few steps forward. "We should check it out. Maybe we'll find supplies."

"Or answers," I added.

He nodded, but I could tell he was still unsettled.

We moved slowly, sticking close together. The village was eerily silent—no wind, no distant animal sounds, just the occasional drip of water from the swamp trees.

A few faded symbols were carved into some of the doorways. They looked like writing, but not any language I recognized.

Jayden stopped to examine one, brushing moss away with his fingertips. "This... looks familiar."

Zack raised an eyebrow. "How?"

"I don't know," Jayden murmured, tilting his head. "I just feel like I've seen these shapes before…"

I frowned, stepping beside him. My fingers traced over the grooves in the wood. And then—

A faint glow.

I yanked my hand back.

The symbol had lit up for a second—just a flicker of golden light before it faded away.

Sofia stepped back. "Okay. Nope. Nope, nope, nope. If the old creepy writing starts glowing, I'm out."

I glanced at Zack, but he looked just as lost as I was.

"What if it's connected to our bracelets?" I said slowly, touching my wrist.

Zack's eyes narrowed. He held up his own bracelet and, hesitantly, placed his hand against another carved marking on the hut beside us.

For a moment—nothing.

Then—

A pulse.

It was faint, barely noticeable, but we all felt it. A small hum, like a distant heartbeat.

Something about this place was connected to us.

Jayden swallowed. "I think… I think whoever lived here knew about the Soul Bands."

Sofia shivered. "Or they were the ones who made them."

A heavy silence fell over us.

I turned toward the largest hut at the center of the village. It looked important.

"We need to search this place," I said firmly. "If there are answers, we'll find them here."

Zack hesitated, but then gave a sharp nod. "Let's go."

And together, we stepped deeper into the lost village.

The moment we stepped past the threshold of the largest hut, something felt different. The air was thicker, like stepping into a room filled with memories that weren't ours. My heart pounded in my chest, my fingers twitching at my sides. Even Cappy, my mechanical monkey, clung closer to my shoulder, his little metal fingers tightening against my jacket.

Zack was the first to step forward, his eyes scanning the space like he expected something to jump out at us. His bird, Ash, let out a quiet squawk and ruffled its metal feathers, sensing the same strange feeling we all did.

Inside, the hut was larger than I expected. The walls were lined with wooden shelves, though most had collapsed under age and rot. Broken clay jars littered the floor, their contents long dried up or turned to dust. A massive table stood in the center of the room, cracked but still standing.

And on the farthest wall—a mural.

It stretched across the entire back of the hut, covered in symbols, painted images, and scenes that I didn't understand but somehow felt important.

Jayden let out a soft gasp. "This... this is history."

Sofia was less impressed. "This is *creepy,*" she muttered, but she still stepped closer, her snake curling protectively around her wrist.

I swallowed hard and traced a hand over one of the paintings. It showed four figures. They weren't detailed—more like silhouettes—but each one was different. One stood with light surrounding them, another held something that looked like a hammer or tool, the third had an outstretched hand to an animal, and the last figure was surrounded by floating objects.

I didn't need to be a genius to see the connection.

"Guys," I whispered. "I think... I think this is us."

Zack stepped beside me, following my gaze. His jaw clenched. "That's not possible. How could they know about us?"

Jayden's eyes flicked from symbol to symbol, his fingers moving as if solving a puzzle in his head. "Maybe it's not about *us,* exactly," he said carefully. "Maybe it's about others who came before us."

My stomach twisted. "You think there were others?"

Sofia huffed, shaking her head. "No way. We would've seen signs of them."

"Would we?" Jayden countered. "We don't know how long ago this village was abandoned. And... well, look at our bracelets."

We all did.

The Soul Bands on our wrists felt heavier.

Cappy gave a little chitter, rubbing his head against my cheek as if to calm me down. Zack shifted uncomfortably, his hand brushing over Ash's metallic wings.

Something big was happening here.

Sofia crossed her arms. "Fine. Let's say someone else was here before us. What happened to them?"

No one had an answer.

Zack exhaled sharply, like he was forcing down his nerves. "We need to keep looking. Maybe there's something here that explains what happened."

I nodded, even though my heart was pounding.

We split up, each of us searching different parts of the hut. I checked the shelves, running my fingers over old, weathered papers that crumbled at my touch. Jayden focused on the mural, trying to decipher more of the symbols.

Zack went for the table.

The moment he touched it, the wood groaned.

"Uh... that's not good," he muttered.

The floor beneath us shuddered.

Sofia yelped as dust rained from the ceiling. I staggered back, nearly tripping over broken pottery.

Jayden turned wide-eyed toward us. "What did you *do?!*"

Zack threw up his hands. "I *barely* touched it!"

Another deep groan.

Then, before we could react, the table split down the

middle. The wood collapsed inward, revealing a hidden compartment.

We all froze.

A soft glow pulsed from within.

Jayden inhaled sharply. "That's... that's the same light the Elemental Stone gives off."

Zack shot him a look. "Then what's it *doing here?*"

Slowly, carefully, I stepped forward and peered inside.

A small crystal sat at the bottom of the hidden space. It wasn't as big as the Elemental Stone, but it had the same shifting, prismatic colors.

I reached for it.

Cappy chittered nervously, but I ignored him, my fingers brushing the crystal's smooth surface.

The moment I touched it, a shock of energy surged through me.

I gasped, staggering back.

For one second, everything changed.

The hut was full again—not broken, not abandoned. The mural was brighter, clearer. And figures—shadowy, unrecognizable—moved around us, their voices overlapping in a language I didn't understand.

Then—it was gone.

I stumbled, breath ragged, my heart hammering against my ribs.

Jayden caught me. "Addy! Are you okay?"

I blinked, my vision still blurry.

Zack and Sofia were staring at me, their faces pale.

"What just happened?" Zack demanded.

I swallowed hard, my fingers still tingling. "I think..." I took a deep breath, looking back at the faintly glowing crystal.

"I think I just saw the past."

CHAPTER 7

ZACK – THE CREATURE OF THE SWAMP

I stared at Addy, my heart pounding in my chest. She was still breathing hard, her fingers trembling after touching the crystal. Whatever she had just seen, it shook her.

Jayden and Sofia were watching her carefully, but my eyes drifted back to the hidden compartment in the broken table. The crystal inside still pulsed softly, a rhythm that felt eerily alive.

"This isn't like the Elemental Stone," I muttered. "It's... different."

Jayden adjusted his glasses, his eyes locked on the glow. "It could be another artifact—one with memories tied to it. If Addy's right, and it let her see the past, then maybe—"

The ground trembled, and the thick, murky water of

the swamp rippled as something massive moved beneath its surface.

I swallowed hard, my fingers tightening around the hilt of my sword. The ruins behind us, the ancient carvings, the eerie silence—it all suddenly made sense. This place wasn't abandoned because people left. Something drove them out.

"Uh... tell me I'm not the only one hearing that," Sofia whispered, taking a cautious step backward. Her mechanical snake slithered tightly around her arm, its glowing eyes flicking toward the shifting water.

"Nope. Definitely not just you," I muttered.

Jayden adjusted his glasses, his free hand resting on Charles's back. The fire-infused raptor crouched low, his glowing red eyes locked on the rippling swamp, his tail flicking anxiously.

Addy lifted a hand, summoning a globe of light to hover above us. The glow flickered against the mist, barely piercing through the thick shadows.

And then, the water exploded.

A massive shape burst from the swamp, a towering, moss-covered beast that looked like it had been stitched together from roots, stone, and sludge. It had four long arms, each ending in razor-sharp claws, and a wide, gaping mouth filled with dripping black fangs. Its eyes burned red, just like the T-Rex back on the beach.

"Oh, that is NOT okay," I said, stumbling back as the monster let out a roar that shook the trees.

It swung one massive arm toward us, and I barely had time to dive out of the way before it smashed into the ruined stone where I had just been standing. Pieces of ancient carvings shattered and flew everywhere.

"Spread out!" Addy shouted, hurling a spear of light at the creature's face.

The attack hit, making the swamp monster stumble back, but it didn't do nearly as much damage as I hoped. The vines and moss regrew, sealing over the burned hole.

"Great," I muttered. "It heals itself. That's fair."

Charles let out a shrill screech and charged forward, dodging between the creature's legs before leaping up and latching onto its side. The raptor's claws dug deep, fire erupting from the wounds as he climbed higher, tearing at the moss and vines.

The monster howled, flailing to shake Charles off.

"He's not gonna be able to hold on for long!" Jayden shouted. He lifted his hands, his Soul Band glowing as he summoned more creatures—a trio of mud-covered swamp lizards that slithered onto the battlefield.

"Keep it busy!" Addy called, forming another spear of light.

I ran, dodging around broken ruins and half-sunken pillars, looking for an opening. If fire worked, maybe I could craft something useful—a trap, a weapon, anything.

"Sofia! Got anything flammable in your inventory?" I called.

She frowned, checking her Soul Band's storage. "Uh...

I've got dried vines, wood, some oil from that weird tree we passed—"

"Oil! Give me that!"

She tossed it to me, and I immediately grabbed some loose fabric, wrapping it around the oil-soaked wood. Then, I focused on my Soul Band, channeling my crafting ability into the materials. The glow surrounded my hands, twisting the components together, melding them into something new.

Torch Spear Created!

I grinned and ignited the tip, turning just in time to see Charles thrown to the ground with a pained screech.

"Jayden, he okay?" I asked, heart racing.

"He's fine—he's getting back up!" Jayden reassured me, though he was clearly rattled. Charles shook himself off and snapped his jaws, glaring at the monster with burning fury.

"Good. Because I think it's time to even the odds."

I ran straight at the monster, gripping the Torch Spear tightly.

"Zack, what are you doing?!" Addy yelled.

The creature reared back one massive arm, ready to swat me away like a fly.

At the last second, I slid under its swing, bringing the flaming spear up and jamming it straight into its chest.

The effect was instant.

Fire spread across its body, crawling up its vines, devouring the moss like dry paper. The monster screamed, staggering backward, thrashing wildly as flames raced along its limbs.

"NOW! HIT IT WITH EVERYTHING YOU GOT!" I shouted.

Addy threw a javelin of light, aiming for the creature's already burning chest. Jayden's summoned lizards latched onto its legs, biting and clawing to keep it unsteady.

Charles launched himself at its back again, this time going straight for the neck. He clamped his powerful jaws down, his fire-infused bite sinking deep.

The monster flailed, screeched, and then... collapsed.

It hit the swamp with a heavy splash, the fire consuming its form until nothing remained but a pile of smoldering vines and cracked stone.

The jungle went silent.

My chest heaved as I caught my breath, my heart still hammering from the fight.

"Well," Sofia muttered, wiping muck off her face, "that was horrifying."

I let out a breathless laugh, dropping onto a fallen log. "Yup. But we won."

Jayden rushed over to Charles, checking the raptor for wounds. "You okay, buddy?"

The raptor huffed, nudging Jayden's arm. His scales still flickered with heat, but he seemed fine.

"I can't believe we just fought a living swamp nightmare," Addy said, looking down at the charred remains.

"It had the same red eyes as the T-Rex. It was definitely controlled by something."

I glanced at the Elemental Stone, still tucked safely in Sofia's hands. "Which means we're still being hunted."

Nobody said anything for a long moment. The weight of that truth settled over us like a thick fog.

"Come on," I finally said, standing up. "Let's get back to the river and keep moving. We need to get to the Crystal Mountain before something even worse finds us."

No one argued.

We gathered our things and made our way back to the raft. The river carried us forward, drifting away from the smoldering remains of the battle.

Ahead, the trees thinned, revealing an open grove bathed in moonlight.

For now, at least, we were safe.

CHAPTER 8
ADDY – OUT OF THE SWAMP

The river carried us far away from the swamp, its once-murky water gradually clearing as we drifted closer to the mountain. The thick humidity that had weighed on our skin for what felt like forever began to thin out, replaced by a cooler breeze that sent a chill down my spine.

I exhaled, feeling some of the tension drain from my shoulders.

"We're actually out," I muttered, half to myself, half to the others.

Jayden, sitting near the front of the raft with Charles, let out a shaky breath. "I was starting to think we never would be." He ran a hand along Charles's back, fingers brushing over the sleek fire-infused feathers that still glowed faintly in the dimming light. "That thing in the swamp... it almost got us."

I shuddered at the memory. The massive creature, its twisting tendrils, the way it manipulated our minds with illusions—I never wanted to go through something like that again.

Sofia hugged herself, rubbing her arms as if shaking off a cold she couldn't feel. "Yeah, well, let's all agree that we're *never* going back there."

"No arguments here," Zack said, adjusting his grip on the long wooden pole he'd been using to help steer the raft. "But let's not forget something—someone was controlling that thing. That's the second time now we've run into something with those red glowing eyes."

He was right. First the T-Rex, now the swamp creature. Both had been aggressive, unnatural, and both had turned normal after the fight ended.

A chill ran down my spine, and not from the air. "It's not a coincidence. Someone—or *something*—doesn't want us reaching Crystal Mountain."

Zack nodded, jaw clenched. "Which means we need to be ready for whatever's waiting for us up there."

The raft bumped against a rocky shore, and I grabbed onto the edge to steady myself. The river had narrowed in the last few miles, funneled between steep cliff walls, and now it finally emptied into a wide clearing at the base of the mountain.

I took a step onto solid ground, nearly sighing in relief as my boots sank into dry soil instead of swamp mud.

"Land!" Sofia declared, dramatically flopping onto the

ground. "Finally, I can *breathe* without it smelling like rotten eggs."

I rolled my eyes but couldn't blame her. The swamp had been oppressive, the air thick and stifling. Here, it felt fresh and clean, like we'd passed through a doorway into a completely different world.

Jayden adjusted his glasses, scanning our surroundings. "We should set up camp here for the night. The sun's going down, and we need to recover before we start the climb."

Zack frowned like he wanted to argue, but even he looked exhausted. His copper armor was scuffed, dirt smeared across his face from the battle earlier.

I crossed my arms and gave him a look. "Don't even try to say we should keep going."

Zack sighed, rubbing the back of his head. "Fine, fine. But first thing in the morning, we move."

We got to work setting up camp, each of us falling into a familiar rhythm. Zack and Jayden worked on building a fire, gathering dry branches while Zack used his crafting ability to form a proper fire pit with stones. Sofia pulled supplies from her inventory, setting out blankets and extra food.

I took the opportunity to check on Cappy, my mechanical monkey. He'd been quiet since the battle, tucked against my shoulder like a comforting weight.

"You okay, buddy?" I asked, running my fingers along the metal plating of his back.

A wave of warmth and reassurance flooded through me, like a mental hug.

I smiled. "Yeah, I'm glad we're out of there too."

As the fire crackled to life, its golden glow flickering against the mountain's shadowy slopes, we finally sat down as a team, letting ourselves *breathe*.

For the first time in what felt like forever, there was a sense of peace.

Zack leaned back on his elbows, staring up at the sky as it darkened into deep purples and blues, the first stars twinkling above.

"You ever think about what happens when we get back?" he asked, voice quieter than usual.

Sofia, who had been chewing on dried fruit, hesitated. "You mean if we get back."

"*When*," I corrected her, firmly. "We *will*."

Sofia sighed. "I dunno. It just... feels like we've been here so long. What if things aren't the same? What if time is different back home?"

Jayden nodded, adjusting his glasses. "I've thought about that too. If no time has passed, then everything just... goes back to normal. But if it's been *weeks*, how do we explain *any of this*?"

The fire popped, sending a shower of sparks into the air.

"I don't think it'll be the same," Zack admitted. "Even if no time has passed, *we've* changed." He glanced down at his Soul Band, his fingers brushing over the Creation

Matrix embedded in his skin. "We're not just normal kids anymore."

A silence settled over us.

We all *felt* it.

This journey—the dangers, the battles, the way we'd been forced to grow and trust each other—it had changed us in ways we couldn't undo.

Sofia pulled her knees to her chest. "I miss my family."

Jayden nodded. "Me too."

I swallowed the lump in my throat. "Same."

Zack looked at me, blue eyes serious and steady. "Then let's get back to them."

I stared at him for a long moment before nodding. "Yeah."

For the next hour, we just talked, sharing stories about home, memories of our families, and all the stupid, normal things we missed.

Sofia missed movie nights with her dad.

Jayden missed his books and quiet afternoons in the library.

I missed cooking with my mom.

Zack, after a long silence, muttered, "I miss *not* messing things up."

I nudged him with my shoulder. "You haven't messed anything up, Zack."

He scoffed. "Oh, please. I was an idiot when we first got here."

"Yeah, you were," I agreed, grinning when he shot me

a look. "But you're not anymore. You learned. You grew. And we trust you."

Zack let out a breath, shaking his head with a small smile. "Well... thanks."

Charles made a low rumbling sound, stretching out beside Jayden, his fire-warmed scales flickering in the dim light.

Cappy curled against my arm, sending another wave of comfort through my mind.

Zack's bird, Ash, fluffed his metallic feathers, hopping closer to Zack's side.

For the first time in a long time, we weren't just surviving.

We were a team.

And tomorrow, we'd climb that mountain—*together*.

CHAPTER 9
ZACK – THE MOUNTAIN CLIMB

The mountain loomed ahead, its jagged peaks piercing the sky like stone blades. The higher we climbed, the more unforgiving the terrain became—jagged rocks, loose gravel, and the ever-present feeling that one wrong step could send us tumbling down the mountainside.

At least we weren't freezing.

Our fire-infused copper armor radiated a steady warmth, pushing away the chilling winds that howled through the cliffs. I ran a gloved hand along my heated chestplate, silently thanking past-Zack for crafting these. Without them, this climb would be miserable.

"Okay," Sofia huffed, adjusting the fire-warmed scarf I made her, "I still hate the cold, but I *guess* this armor is making it bearable."

"Glad to know my genius is finally getting recognized," I smirked.

Addy, walking ahead, shot me a side-eye. *"Finally?* You *just* started listening to other people."

I held up my hands, grinning. "Okay, okay, fair point."

Jayden, walking beside Charles, was still adjusting to his armor's heat. He loosened the straps around his neck and shook his head. "I think mine is *too* warm."

Charles let out a snorting sound, as if laughing at him. The fire-infused raptor had zero issues with the heat. In fact, he looked completely at home, his scales shimmering between deep green and fiery red, his warm breath visible in the cold air.

"You could turn yours down if you focused," I told Jayden. "Just think about lowering the intensity. It's tied to the Elemental Stone's power, so it should respond."

Jayden frowned, staring down at his bracelet, before closing his eyes in concentration. A moment later, the heat coming from his armor dialed back slightly.

He opened his eyes, surprised. "Huh. That actually worked."

"Of course it did," I said, pretending like I totally knew that would happen and wasn't just guessing.

"Less talking, more climbing," Addy said, keeping a steady pace ahead.

We followed, footsteps crunching over loose gravel. The incline grew steeper, and soon, we had to start using our hands to climb over rocky ledges. The wind howled, sending loose pebbles tumbling down the cliffside.

After about an hour of climbing, we hit our first real obstacle.

A narrow stone bridge, barely wide enough for one person at a time, stretched across a deep chasm. The bridge looked old, with cracks running through its surface, and a strong gust of wind could send anyone toppling over the side.

"Oh, no," Sofia said immediately, shaking her head. "*Nope.* Not doing it. Not crossing that. No way."

"We *have* to," Addy said, examining the bridge with a critical eye. "It's either this, or we go back and find another way."

Jayden pulled out the map. "There *isn't* another way," he said. "This is the only path that leads straight up to the next plateau."

Sofia crossed her arms, glaring at the bridge. "That thing looks like it's gonna collapse if a *butterfly* lands on it."

I knelt down and tapped the bridge. It held, but there was definitely some give. Not ideal.

"...We can reinforce it," I said, gears turning in my head. "Give me a sec."

Pulling materials from my pouch, I quickly crafted support beams from copper and stone, anchoring them into the most cracked sections of the bridge. It wouldn't make it indestructible, but it should hold under our weight.

Sofia still didn't look convinced.

"Sofia," I said, putting a hand on her shoulder, "you trust me, right?"

She looked at me, then at the bridge, then groaned dramatically. "Fine. But if I *die*, I'm haunting you."

I grinned. "Noted."

One by one, we crossed the bridge, moving carefully. Addy went first, using her light powers to create small glowing markers on the safest footholds. Jayden followed, Charles jumping across with surprising agility.

Then it was my turn. I stepped slowly, testing each step before putting my full weight down. The reinforcements held, but I still felt a few unsettling shifts beneath me.

Sofia was right behind me, moving slower than all of us.

"You're doing great," I called over my shoulder.

"Shut up," she muttered, concentrating hard.

We were almost across when I heard it.

A low growl.

Charles suddenly whipped his head around, his tail lashing, sensing something before we did.

Then—movement.

Something huge emerged from a cave along the cliffside.

A mountain beast.

It looked like a massive panther, but its fur blended into the rocks, making it almost invisible. Its golden eyes locked onto us.

It crouched low, muscles coiling—

Then it leapt.

Right onto the bridge.

The stone cracked beneath its weight.

Sofia screamed, nearly losing her balance.

"GO!" I shouted, pushing forward as the bridge began to crumble.

Addy launched a hard light javelin, hitting the beast square in the chest, knocking it back slightly—but not enough.

Jayden whistled, and Charles sprang into action, slamming into the creature midair.

But the bridge wasn't going to hold.

A section collapsed behind Sofia—and she was trapped.

"I— I can't—" she gasped, staring at the gap between her and the rest of us.

"Jump!" I yelled. "I'll catch you!"

Her eyes darted to the massive drop below.

"I *can't*!"

The mountain beast roared, shaking off Charles, preparing to pounce again.

I didn't have time to argue.

I ripped off my belt, threw it toward her. "*Grab on!*"

She latched onto it, and I hauled her forward, pulling her across the gap.

She crashed into me, knocking us both to the ground just as the last of the bridge gave way.

The mountain beast fell with it, letting out a final, echoing roar before disappearing into the abyss.

We laid there, panting, hearts racing.

Sofia buried her face in my chestplate, muttering, "*I hate mountains. I hate everything.*"

I just laughed breathlessly. "That was *awesome.*"

Addy grabbed my arm, pulling me up. "We need to move. That *wasn't* the last thing we'll face up here."

She was right.

We weren't at the top yet.

And something told me that this was just the beginning of what the mountain had in store for us.

CHAPTER 10
ADDY - THE CAVE
OF WHISPERS

The wind howled like a living thing, cutting through the mountain pass and forcing us forward. It was getting late, and though the enchanted warmth of our armor kept us from freezing, exhaustion still weighed down every step.

Ahead, a dark opening yawned against the rocky cliffside—a cave.

"There!" I called, pointing toward it. "We can rest there for the night."

"Are you sure?" Zack asked, stepping up beside me. His breath came in short bursts, his face streaked with dirt. "What if there's *another* monster inside?"

"We'll deal with it," I said, determined. "We need to rest, Zack. We can't climb through the night."

Jayden pulled out the map, eyes scanning over the markings. "I don't see anything about a cave here, but that's not surprising. The map has been incomplete before."

Sofia wrapped her arms around herself, looking warily at the cave entrance. "As long as it doesn't try to *eat* us, I'm fine with it."

Charles sniffed the air and let out a soft chuff, as if warning us to be on guard.

That made me hesitate.

But what choice did we have?

The wind was picking up, and night was coming fast.

I tightened my grip on my spear of light and took the first step inside.

The moment we entered, everything changed.

At first, the cave seemed normal enough—damp rock, a few scattered stalactites overhead, and a twisting path that led deeper inside. My glowing orb of light illuminated the uneven walls, casting flickering shadows as we walked forward.

Then, I heard it.

A whisper.

Soft. Indistinct.

It slithered through the cave like a breath of wind, just barely brushing against my ears.

I turned sharply, heart pounding. "Did you hear that?"

"Hear what?" Zack asked.

More whispers.

Low, hissing words, just at the edge of understanding.

Jayden tensed. "I hear it too."

Charles let out a low growl, his head darting around as if searching for an unseen enemy.

The whispers grew louder.

I spun around, trying to find the source, but there was nothing—only the cave, stretching endlessly into darkness.

Then, the words became clear.

And I felt my blood turn to ice.

"They don't trust you, Addy."

I froze.

The voice wasn't random. It was targeting me.

"They think you're bossy. Controlling. They follow Zack because they don't want to follow you."

No. That wasn't true.

Was it?

I clenched my fists. "Stop," I whispered, shaking my head. "You're just—just a stupid cave."

But the whispers didn't stop.

"He thinks he's better than you. Zack wants to lead because he doesn't think you're strong enough."

I turned, eyes locking on Zack.

He was frowning, shifting uncomfortably—he was hearing something too.

Then, he spoke. "Why would you *say* that?"

I blinked. "Say *what*?"

His blue eyes narrowed. "You said I wasn't a *real leader*."

"I *never* said that!" I snapped.

But Zack didn't look convinced.

And suddenly, I realized what was happening.

The cave wasn't just whispering.

It was twisting our fears against us.

I saw the moment Sofia's face paled, her hands curling into fists.

"They think you're useless. All you do is carry things."

Her eyes darted between us, her breathing shaky.

Jayden, standing stiffly beside Charles, suddenly looked furious.

"They don't respect you, Jayden. They think you're just the nerd—only good for figuring out puzzles. They don't care what you want."

His shoulders tensed.

The cave wanted us to fight.

To tear each other apart.

And for a second—it was working.

No.

I wouldn't let this happen.

We'd been through too much. We weren't going to fall apart now.

I gritted my teeth, drew my light into my hands, and let it flare outward.

"ENOUGH!"

The light burst, illuminating the entire cave—and for a brief moment, I saw them.

Shadowy figures, shifting in the darkness, retreating from the glow.

The whispers screamed—then faded.

Breathing hard, I turned to my friends.

Zack's fists were clenched. Sofia looked near tears. Jayden's jaw was tight, his glasses slightly fogged from his breathing.

But we were still here.

Still together.

I swallowed hard and forced my voice to stay steady.

"That wasn't *us*," I said, looking at each of them. "It was *this cave*. Trying to mess with us."

Zack rubbed the back of his neck. "I—I know. I just —" He let out a breath. "I thought for a second—"

Sofia wiped at her eyes. "It sounded *so real*."

Jayden pushed his glasses up. "It was feeding on our insecurities. Our doubts. That's why it felt so convincing."

I nodded. "But it's *not* true. None of it is."

I took a step forward, staring each of them in the eye.

"Zack—you're a great leader, and you *listen* to us. More than you think. We chose you because we trust you."

Zack hesitated—then nodded, his expression softening.

"Sofia—your inventory skill has saved us more times than I can count. You're so much more than just a storage unit."

Sofia sniffed. "I *guess* you're right."

Jayden exhaled, rubbing his forehead. "And I *know* I'm more than just the nerd. You guys always listen to me when it matters."

I smiled. "Exactly."

The tension broke.

And suddenly, we weren't four people caught in a nightmare.

We were a team again.

I turned to Charles, running a hand over his scaled head. "You sensed it, didn't you?"

The raptor nuzzled into my touch, letting out a soft huff—almost like a purr.

Our companions—Cappy, Ash, Neil, and Sofia's snake—had all been unusually quiet, but now they slowly came forward, pressing against us.

A soft, comforting warmth spread through me.

They'd been fighting it, too.

Maybe even helping us resist.

I took a deep breath. "We're okay."

Zack stretched his arms, shaking off the last of the unease. "We should probably sleep in shifts, though. Just in case."

"Agreed," Jayden said.

We settled in, the cave still and silent now.

And as I stared up at the dark ceiling, I whispered, just loud enough for myself to hear—

"We're stronger than you think."

CHAPTER 11
ZACK – THE BRIDGE OF FATE

The wind howled through the chasm like a ghostly warning. I stood at the edge of the drop, my breath catching as I peered down into the abyss. The ground beneath us had given way to a massive gorge, its jagged walls stretching far below into shifting mist. I had no way of telling just how deep it went, but my gut told me one wrong step and we'd never find out the bottom firsthand.

What lay before us was the only way across—an ancient, narrow bridge, weathered by time and barely holding together. Thick ropes, frayed at the edges, stretched between rickety wooden planks, some of which had rotted completely through.

"This is a joke, right?" Sofia said, stepping up beside me. Her voice was laced with nervous disbelief as she eyed the bridge. "We're not actually going to cross *that*, are we?"

Jayden adjusted his glasses and squinted at the structure. "It's old, but if it's lasted this long, it might still be stable."

"Or," Sofia said dryly, "it might collapse the second we step on it."

I exhaled, gripping my sword hilt for reassurance. "We don't have a choice. The path stops here. We either cross, or we turn back."

Addy walked forward, testing the first plank with her foot. It creaked, but held firm. "We should go one at a time. Spread out the weight."

That made sense, but I could already tell no one was eager to volunteer.

Even Charles hesitated, his raptor instincts probably screaming at him to avoid something this unstable.

Jayden was the first to break the silence. "I can try to reinforce it. Maybe if I direct some of Charles' flames at the ropes, I can harden them—make them stronger."

I nodded. "Do it."

Jayden pressed a hand to Charles' side, eyes narrowing in concentration. "Okay, buddy," he whispered. "Controlled fire, just enough heat."

Charles let out a low chuff, then opened his mouth and sent a stream of controlled flames along the ropes. The heat didn't burn them, but instead seemed to fuse and strengthen the fibers, solidifying the weakened areas. The planks even seemed a little less fragile.

Sofia exhaled. "I *really* hope that worked."

I smirked at her. "Guess we'll find out."

Without waiting for more objections, I stepped onto the bridge first.

The moment my weight settled, the bridge swayed.

My heart jumped into my throat. I dug my fingers into the ropes and took slow, careful steps, keeping my weight balanced.

Each plank groaned beneath my boots, but they held.

"Okay," I called back. "One at a time, just like we said."

Addy went next, keeping a firm grip on the ropes as she followed behind me. Jayden came after, with Sofia muttering about how unfair life was before stepping on herself.

Charles, however, stayed back.

I turned to Jayden. "You think he can cross?"

Jayden bit his lip. "His weight might be a problem."

"Maybe he can jump across?" Addy suggested.

"Too risky," Jayden said, shaking his head. "If he misses—"

"Then I *don't* miss."

We all froze.

The voice hadn't come from any of us.

It came from behind us.

I turned my head slowly, gripping my sword as a shadow moved in the mist at the edge of the cliff.

Then, a figure stepped forward.

A boy.

I barely had time to register his features before Charles let out a deep, warning growl.

The stranger didn't flinch.

He looked to be our age, maybe a little older, with wild black hair that stuck up in messy spikes and sharp green eyes that gleamed in the dim light. His clothes were worn and tattered, like he'd been out here for a long time.

But the most important thing?

He had a Soul Band on his wrist.

Just like us.

"Who are you?" I demanded.

The boy smirked. "That's a loaded question."

Sofia's grip tightened on the ropes. "You're like us. You have a bracelet."

The boy glanced down at it, as if remembering it was there. "Yeah. Had it for a while now."

Jayden narrowed his eyes. "How long is *a while*?"

The boy didn't answer right away. Instead, he looked past us, at the bridge. "You should get moving. If the storm rolls in before you're across, you won't make it."

I blinked. "Storm?"

He pointed behind us.

I turned—and my stomach dropped.

Dark clouds were rolling in fast, swirling over the chasm with a strange, unnatural energy.

"This island doesn't like when people hesitate," the boy said, grinning. "You either move forward or you get swallowed up."

Addy's voice was sharp. "And why should we trust *you*?"

He tilted his head. "You shouldn't. But since you *will* die if you don't cross soon, that kind of makes the choice easy, doesn't it?"

I clenched my jaw. Something about him felt off, but he wasn't wrong about the storm.

"Go," I told the others. "Hurry."

One by one, we rushed forward, our steps quick but careful. The bridge swayed wildly as the wind picked up, but we kept moving.

Charles let out a frustrated screech, pacing at the edge of the chasm.

"He's not going to make it across like that," Jayden said, his voice panicked.

"Then I'll help," the boy said, stepping forward.

Jayden immediately put himself between him and Charles. "Help *how*?"

The boy smirked. "I can *command* him across."

That set off every alarm in my head.

Jayden's face darkened. "You mean control him."

The boy rolled his eyes. "Look, do you want your dino-dragon to make it or not?"

I gritted my teeth.

Then the storm howled, lightning crackling in the sky, and I realized—

We were out of time.

"Fine," I snapped. "Do it. But if you hurt him—"

The boy held up his hands innocently. "Relax."

He took one step forward, lifted his hand, and suddenly—

Charles leaped onto the bridge.

He bounded forward, his movements unnaturally precise, like someone had flipped a switch in his brain.

Jayden tensed, eyes wide with conflicted horror.

I didn't like this. Not one bit.

But Charles crossed the bridge safely, landing beside us just as the first crack of thunder rumbled overhead.

The boy grinned. "See? Easy."

Then he jumped—not onto the bridge, but straight over the chasm.

And landed on the other side like it was nothing.

Sofia gasped. "What—what *was that?*"

The boy stretched his arms over his head, looking entirely unbothered.

Then he turned to us and smirked.

"You guys really are slow. You're never gonna make it to the mountain at this rate."

I took a step forward, my pulse pounding.

"Who *are* you?"

The boy grinned wider.

Then he raised his wrist—his Soul Band flickering with energy.

"Let's just say I was here long before you were."

CHAPTER 12
ADDY – THE GUARDIAN'S CHALLENGE

The boy's smirk widened as he stepped forward, his green eyes gleaming with something unreadable. He rolled his shoulders like a fighter preparing for a match, then cracked his knuckles.

"You made it across," he said, tilting his head as he looked at us. "Not bad. Most don't."

I swallowed, my heart still pounding from the bridge crossing. The way he'd commanded Charles with ease, the way he'd leaped the chasm like gravity meant nothing to him—he was not normal.

And now, he was blocking our way forward.

I stepped up beside Zack, gripping my spear of light a little tighter. Something about this boy felt... off.

"Who are you?" I asked, my voice steady despite the unease creeping into my gut.

"I told you," he said, his smirk never fading. "I've been here longer than you."

Jayden moved beside me, placing a protective hand on Charles' side. The raptor let out a low, cautious growl. He didn't trust the boy either.

"What do you want?" Jayden asked, his voice careful.

The boy laughed, the sound casual—almost friendly.

"What I *want*," he said, "doesn't matter. What *you* want, though... now *that's* interesting."

Sofia crossed her arms. "Oh, let me guess. We can't pass unless we beat you in some kind of challenge?"

His grin sharpened. "Ding, ding. We have a winner."

Sofia groaned, throwing up her hands. "This island is literally the worst."

Zack sighed. "Alright. What's the challenge?"

The boy spread his arms wide. "Simple."

A gust of wind kicked up, swirling dust around his feet.

"You want to reach the Crystal Mountain? Prove you deserve to."

Before we could react, the ground beneath us trembled.

Shadows stretched and twisted, coiling around his arms like living things.

His Soul Band glowed.

"Come on then," he said, his voice shifting, taking on a deeper, almost ethereal tone.

"Show me what you've got."

He moved first.

A pulse of dark energy shot from his hands, racing toward us like a tidal wave of shadows.

I barely had time to react.

I threw up a hard-light shield, gritting my teeth as the force slammed into it. The impact sent me skidding backward, my boots struggling to hold traction.

Jayden called out a command, and Charles sprang into action, flames erupting from his maw to counter the darkness.

The fire met the shadows with a violent clash, hissing as they collided.

Zack grabbed my arm, steadying me as I caught my breath. "We need a plan."

"No kidding," I muttered.

The boy laughed again, as if he was actually having *fun*.

"You guys are quick," he said, rolling his neck. "But let's see if you can *keep up*."

Then he vanished.

My breath hitched.

"What—?"

Before I could even finish the thought, he reappeared behind us.

Jayden barely had time to react.

The boy swung a fist, and a blast of wind sent Jayden flying backward.

"Jayden!" Sofia yelled.

She rushed toward him, but the boy wasn't done.

He lifted his hand, and dark chains shot from the ground, wrapping around her legs before she could reach Jayden.

She screamed, struggling against them.

Zack moved fast, his sword flashing in the light as he sliced through the shadows holding her down.

She stumbled free, breathing hard. "I *hate* this guy!"

I clenched my jaw, summoning a light javelin into my hands.

Fine.

If he wanted a fight, he'd get one.

I launched the javelin, aiming straight for his chest.

He dodged—barely.

The light sliced through his sleeve, leaving behind a faint glowing burn.

He paused, looking down at the wound.

Then, to my absolute horror, he grinned wider.

"That's more like it," he said, his eyes gleaming.

Then he vanished again.

Think, Addy, think.

We were reacting, not fighting smart.

He was too fast, too unpredictable.

We needed to outmaneuver him.

I turned to Zack, my mind racing.

"We need to box him in," I said. "If we can control the space, we can force him where we want him."

Zack's eyes lit up. "I have an idea."

He pulled out materials from his pack, his fingers moving fast as he worked.

I had no idea what he was making, but I trusted him.

Meanwhile, Jayden had recovered, and he was guiding Charles forward, his raptor's eyes locked onto the boy's movements.

I turned back to our opponent.

"Hey!" I called. "If you're so tough, why don't you fight us fair?"

He laughed. "What's fair about anything on this island?"

But I noticed something.

He was watching me closely now.

Which meant I had his attention.

Perfect.

I launched forward, striking fast with my spear.

He dodged, but this time, I was ready.

I twisted mid-step, forming another javelin and throwing it at his back.

He turned just in time, but it still clipped his shoulder.

He staggered—just a fraction.

And in that split second—

Zack finished his trap.

The ground beneath the boy lit up.

Glowing runes appeared, forming a tight circle around him.

He froze.

"...Oh."

His smirk finally dropped.

Zack grinned. "Gotcha."

With a snap of his fingers, the trap activated.

Metal sprang up from the ground, forming barriers that caged the boy in on all sides.

He whipped around, his hands glowing with dark energy.

But before he could counter—

Jayden stepped forward.

"Charles," he said.

And Charles unleashed a massive burst of fire.

The flames engulfed the entire trap, forcing the boy backward.

He shielded himself, his own power countering the fire—but he was no longer on offense.

He was trapped.

And finally, he knew it.

The flames died down, and he exhaled slowly, his hands lowering.

Then, to my utter shock, he grinned.

"Well," he said, dusting himself off. "That was impressive."

We stared at him, breathless, still poised to fight.

But he just laughed, running a hand through his messy hair.

"You guys," he said, shaking his head. "You're *actually* fun."

I scowled. "We're not here to entertain you."

He chuckled, then tilted his head thoughtfully.

"...I suppose not," he admitted. "And you did beat me, so..."

He gestured behind him.

The air shifted, and a new path revealed itself—one that hadn't been there before.

"Guess that means you passed."

I exhaled.

Zack lowered his sword.

Jayden glanced between us, then at Charles, who let out a final huff of victory.

Sofia, panting, crossed her arms.

"...That's *it*?"

The boy winked.

"For now."

Then, before we could say anything else, he vanished into the shadows.

Leaving us alone—

With nothing but the open path ahead.

CHAPTER 13
ZACK - THE FINAL ASCENT

The moment the Guardian vanished, leaving nothing but a gust of wind and the faint shimmer of magic in the air, I let out a breath I hadn't realized I was holding. My legs ached, my fingers still tingled from gripping my sword too tight, and my heart pounded like a drum in my chest. But we'd done it.

We won.

I turned to look at my friends. Jayden was holding Charles by the snout, keeping the raptor from pacing anxiously, while Sofia leaned against a boulder, her snake coiled tightly around her arm. Addy, standing beside me, had her spear of light resting against her shoulder, her expression unreadable as she stared up the final stretch of the mountain.

Beyond the bridge, the path was clear—clear, but not easy. The incline grew steep, almost vertical in places, jagged cliffs jutting out like broken teeth. It was a brutal climb, but we were so close. Crystal Mountain loomed above us, its peak glistening in the light, the glow of the Elemental Stone in Sofia's bag pulsing faintly, as if calling to it.

"Alright, team," I said, clapping my hands together to shake off the exhaustion. "No stopping now. This is it. One last push."

Addy nodded, tightening the straps on her armor. "We keep a steady pace, no rushing. I don't want to have to use my light to pull anyone back from a fall."

Jayden adjusted his glasses. "I estimate a few hours of climbing, given the elevation shift and our current level of stamina."

Sofia groaned. "Great. More climbing."

I grinned. "Come on, fancy feet. You handled the bridge, you can handle this."

She shot me a glare but didn't argue.

With one last deep breath, we started up the mountain.

The first stretch was rough, but not impossible. We used the natural handholds where we could, Sofia and I working together to fasten climbing ropes made from vines we found along the path. I even used my crafting skill to reinforce them with hardened fibers, making them stronger. Addy climbed fast, her balance perfect, while Jayden and Charles stuck close together, the raptor's claws finding purchase where our boots struggled.

But the higher we climbed, the worse it got.

The air thinned, making it harder to breathe. The wind picked up, howling against the cliffs, threatening to knock us off our footholds. Even our enchanted copper armor, infused with fire to keep us warm, could only do so much against the biting cold.

At one point, we reached a narrow ledge barely wide enough for us to walk across single file. Below, nothing but a steep drop into the fog-covered valley.

"I hate this," Sofia muttered, hugging the rock wall as she shuffled forward.

"You're doing great," Addy reassured her, already halfway across.

I went last, keeping an eye on Jayden and Charles, making sure neither slipped. My fingers were numb from gripping the rock so hard, my heart hammering in my ears.

Just a little further.

Then the mountain decided to make things harder.

A deep, guttural *crack* echoed through the air. The rock beneath Jayden's foot shifted. His eyes went wide.

"Jayden, jump!" I shouted.

He didn't hesitate. As the ledge crumbled, he leapt forward, landing hard against the cliffside. He scrabbled for a grip, fingers clawing at the stone. Charles screeched, trying to follow, but the raptor wasn't as lucky. His claws skidded off the rock, and suddenly he was falling.

"No!" Jayden screamed.

Without thinking, I dove forward, reaching out. Ash,

my mechanical bird, darted from my shoulder in a blur of silver. He swooped under Charles, flapping wildly, slowing his fall just enough for me to reach him.

I grabbed onto Charles' front limb with both hands, my boots barely holding onto the ledge. The weight almost yanked me off, but Jayden lunged forward, catching my arm.

"Hold on!" he gritted through clenched teeth, struggling to keep both of us from falling.

Addy and Sofia were already moving. Addy summoned a rope of light, wrapping it around my waist to pull me back up. Sofia scrambled over, gripping Jayden's other arm, her snake tightening around her for balance.

With one final pull, we managed to haul Charles back onto the ledge. The moment we were safe, I collapsed, panting hard, my arms burning.

"Too close," I wheezed.

Jayden wrapped his arms around Charles, hugging him fiercely. "I thought I lost you."

Charles let out a low, grumbling sound and nuzzled Jayden's side, clearly shaken but okay.

I turned to Ash, who landed on my shoulder and nudged his metallic beak against my cheek. "Good job, buddy. That was—" I let out a breath. "That was amazing."

Ash cooed softly, the soothing wave of calm he always gave me helping to steady my nerves.

Sofia flopped onto the ground next to me. "I am *so* done with mountains."

Addy just shook her head. "We still have to reach the top."

Sofia groaned, but she didn't argue.

After that, we moved slower, more careful. The mountain wasn't going to make this easy. The final stretch was the worst—rocky, unstable, with jagged spikes of crystal jutting from the stone like glass shards.

The wind howled, strong enough that we had to crouch in places to avoid being knocked off balance. At one point, a small avalanche of loose stones forced us to take cover behind a boulder.

But we didn't stop.

Together, we climbed, hand over hand, foot over foot, pushing forward. Addy led the way, her light guiding us. Jayden used his knowledge of balance and pressure points to pick the safest routes. Sofia, despite her complaining, was quick and agile, finding footholds the rest of us missed. And me—I made sure the ropes held, reinforced the climbing gear, and kept everyone moving.

Then, finally—*finally*—we reached a flat plateau near the summit.

Panting, we collapsed onto solid ground, staring up at the peak of Crystal Mountain.

"We made it," Addy whispered.

Above us, the clouds swirled, the faint glow of the

Elemental Stone growing stronger, as if the mountain itself was calling to it.

I sat up, looking at my friends. We were tired, battered, and worn down—but we were still together.

I grinned. "One more push, guys. Let's finish this."

But as I said the words, a rumble shook the mountain.

And above us, dark clouds began to gather.

A storm was coming.

And something told me this was no ordinary storm.

CHAPTER 14
ADDY – THE STORM

The wind picked up first.

A low howl rolled through the air, whipping at my hair and making my cloak snap behind me. The sky darkened unnaturally fast, clouds gathering above us like a living thing, twisting and curling around the peak of Crystal Mountain. Lightning flashed, but it wasn't the kind I'd seen in normal storms—it was purple, crackling in jagged patterns across the sky, like veins of raw energy breaking apart the atmosphere.

I didn't like this. Not one bit.

"We need to move," I said, my voice tight. "Now."

Sofia hugged her arms, looking up at the sky. "I don't think this storm is... normal."

Jayden adjusted his glasses, pressing himself closer to Charles, whose tail twitched in nervous agitation. "It feels... magical."

"No kidding," Zack muttered, his fingers flexing over the hilt of his sword.

A gust of wind slammed into us, nearly knocking me off my feet. I braced myself, throwing up a light shield just in time to block a flurry of ice shards that came flying from the air. They clattered against the golden barrier, melting the moment they touched its surface.

Ice? From the sky?

I tightened my grip on my magic. "Something isn't right. This storm is *targeting* us."

As if to prove my point, the ground rumbled beneath us, and another bolt of that eerie purple lightning struck the ledge just behind us. The stone cracked, crumbling away into the abyss below. I swallowed hard.

We were running out of mountain.

"We need cover!" Zack shouted over the wind. "We won't last long out here!"

Jayden pointed ahead. "There's a rock outcrop over there! It might give us some shelter!"

It wasn't much—a jagged cluster of boulders jutting out from the mountainside—but it was better than nothing. I nodded. "Go, now!"

Sofia went first, ducking low and running against the wind. Zack followed, using his enhanced crafting ability to reinforce the ground beneath them as they went, making sure no more loose rock would fall under their feet. Jayden and Charles ran next, the raptor pressing close to his side to shield him from the worst of the wind.

I was about to follow when a *boom* louder than anything I'd ever heard split the sky.

The world went white.

Pain shot through my body as I hit the ground, my ears ringing. My vision swam, bright spots dancing in front of me. For a second, I had no idea where I was.

Then I realized—lightning had struck *right next to me.*

Strong hands grabbed me under the arms and hauled me up. "Come on, Addy, move!" Zack shouted, his face pale, eyes wide.

Dizzy, I stumbled forward, forcing my legs to move. The wind screamed around us, dust and debris flying through the air like tiny knives. I gritted my teeth, summoning a shield around us just as another bolt of lightning came crashing down. The energy slammed against my magic, sending a jolt through my body like static electricity. I gasped but held firm.

We made it to the outcrop just in time.

I collapsed onto my knees, panting. My fingers were trembling. That... that was too close.

Jayden helped me sit up, his face worried. "Are you okay?"

"I'm fine," I said, shaking off the lingering shock. I wasn't fine, not really, but we had bigger problems.

The storm wasn't letting up.

The wind howled, whipping around us like an angry beast. Flashes of purple lightning struck the mountain again and again, as if something—*or someone*—was trying to stop us from reaching the summit.

"We can't stay here forever," Sofia said, her voice barely audible over the storm.

I swallowed hard, trying to think. We needed a plan. A way to push forward.

Then, an idea struck me.

"The storm is magical," I said, pushing myself up. "Which means magic should be able to counter it."

Zack looked at me like I'd lost my mind. "You're saying we can *fight a storm*?"

"I'm saying we can *redirect* it," I corrected, clenching my fists. "If we combine our abilities, we might be able to hold it back long enough to make it to the top."

Jayden looked thoughtful. "I think she's right. Weather magic is complex, but if we disrupt the flow of energy in the storm, it might weaken."

"I can use my light to create a shield against the wind and lightning," I said. "Zack, if you can craft barriers out of stone, it'll reinforce my shield."

Sofia caught on quickly. "And I can use my ability to sense elemental energy to help us find a break in the storm."

Jayden straightened, confidence growing in his expression. "If I focus, I might be able to connect with Charles and get a sense of where the safest path is."

We exchanged a look.

It was risky.

But we didn't have a choice.

I took a deep breath and reached for my power. A golden barrier of light stretched out from my hands, forming a dome over us. Zack slammed his palms against the ground, channeling his crafting ability into the stone, reinforcing my shield with solid rock.

Sofia closed her eyes, reaching out with her magic. "There! To the right! The storm is weaker that way!"

Jayden pressed his forehead to Charles' snout, murmuring something to him. After a moment, the raptor let out a sharp chirp, then darted ahead, leading the way.

We ran.

The wind fought us every step of the way, tearing at our clothes, trying to pull us back. Lightning struck the barrier again and again, each hit sending a shockwave through my magic. My arms ached, my legs burned, but I didn't stop. Zack was right beside me, keeping the barrier strong. Sofia called out directions, guiding us through the worst of the storm. Jayden and Charles led the charge, moving quickly over the unstable terrain.

Step by step, we pushed forward.

Then—just as suddenly as it had begun—the storm broke.

The wind died down. The lightning stopped.

We stumbled to a halt, gasping for breath.

I looked up.

The summit of Crystal Mountain was just ahead.

We had made it.

But as we took in the sight before us, my stomach twisted.

The top of the mountain wasn't empty.

Something—*or someone*—was waiting for us.

CHAPTER 15
ZACK – THE CRYSTAL CAVERN

I wiped the sweat from my brow and took a deep breath, staring ahead at the summit that loomed just beyond our reach. We were so close—closer than we'd ever been. After everything we'd fought through, every danger we'd survived, the Elemental Stone's resting place was within sight.

But first, there was this cavern.

A massive opening in the side of the mountain yawned before us, lined with jagged crystal formations that pulsed faintly in the dim light. The air was charged with energy, making the hairs on my arms stand up. I had a feeling that whatever was inside wasn't just going to be a pretty collection of gems.

"I don't like this," Sofia said, hugging her arms as she stared at the cave's glowing entrance. "Why does it feel like it's... watching us?"

Charles growled low in his throat, shifting uneasily beside Jayden. The raptor's feathers fluffed up, his fiery orange streaks glowing faintly in the crystal light.

"Because it's full of magic," Addy murmured, stepping closer and running a hand along one of the crystals near the entrance. "It's like... it's alive."

I felt it too. The same tingle of energy I'd sensed in the Elemental Stone, only stronger—more intense. Whatever these crystals were, they weren't ordinary.

Jayden adjusted his glasses and knelt to examine one of the smaller clusters growing from the rock. "These formations... I've read about things like this before. Some believe certain crystals can hold magical energy. But these—" He hesitated, glancing up at me. "These feel ancient. As if they've been absorbing power for centuries."

I swallowed, my fingers tightening around the hilt of my sword. "Only one way to find out what they do."

We stepped inside.

The moment we crossed the threshold, the air shifted. A soft hum filled my ears, like the mountain itself was singing. The crystals along the walls glowed brighter, casting shimmering reflections against the stone floor. The deeper we went, the more intense the energy became, pressing against my skin like a living force.

Then, the magic *reacted*.

A pulse of energy rippled through the cavern. Light flared from the crystals, and suddenly, a floating image formed in the air before us—a moving, shifting swirl of colors and shapes.

A vision.

It showed people—figures wrapped in long robes, their hands outstretched toward a massive, glowing crystal at the center of the cavern. Magic streamed from their fingertips, intertwining with the light of the crystal. The air crackled with power, and I realized with a jolt—

They were creating the Elemental Stone.

I stepped forward, barely breathing as the vision shifted. The crystal at the center of the cavern shone brighter, and for a moment, I swore I saw the same swirling energy I'd felt when I held the stone myself.

"They made it here," Addy whispered beside me. "The Elemental Stone... was *forged* here."

Sofia pressed a hand to her chest. "But why? What did they use it for?"

The vision changed again. Shadows crept in, swirling around the figures in robes. Their magic faltered, the light dimming as dark shapes loomed over them. I tensed. Whatever had happened next, it hadn't been good.

The crystal cracked.

The robed figures recoiled, their expressions filled with horror as fractures split through the great stone. Energy exploded outward, sending them flying. The vision blurred, shifting into chaos—shadows overtaking the cavern, the crystal splintering into shards, and finally—

A portal.

It flashed open in the middle of the cavern, swirling with the same purple energy we'd seen in the storm. The robed figures staggered toward it, some vanishing into the light while others remained behind, desperately trying to contain whatever had been unleashed.

Then, the vision *ended*.

The cavern fell silent.

I let out a shaky breath, my mind racing. "They didn't just make the Elemental Stone," I said, piecing it together. "They used it to *open something*."

Jayden rubbed his temple, clearly overwhelmed. "It must have been a portal—to another realm, another world. But something went wrong."

Addy crossed her arms, her expression grim. "And if the stone was made here, that means returning it could either fix what they broke... or finish what they started."

The weight of her words sank into me. This wasn't just about getting home. This wasn't even about returning the Elemental Stone. Whatever we were doing... *it was bigger than us*.

"We need to keep moving," I said firmly. "The answers we need are at the summit."

Sofia hesitated. "And if the answers are something we don't want to hear?"

I clenched my jaw. "Then we'll figure it out. *Together*."

She nodded, and we all turned toward the cavern's exit. As we passed the glowing crystals, I felt their energy hum beneath my fingertips, as if they were whispering secrets just beyond my understanding.

We were almost there.

And I had a feeling the hardest part of our journey was still ahead.

CHAPTER 16
ADDY – THE REVELATION

The wind howled as we stepped out of the crystal cavern and onto a narrow path that led up the final stretch of Crystal Mountain. My heart pounded, not just from the altitude but from what we had seen. The visions in the cave had changed everything.

The Elemental Stone wasn't just a key to getting home. It was a piece of something much bigger—something ancient, powerful, and maybe even dangerous.

I clutched it in my hand, feeling the warmth pulsing from within. It almost felt *alive*.

"Are we sure about this?" Sofia asked, glancing at me with uncertainty. "If we put the stone back, what if... what if it doesn't take us home? What if it does something worse?"

I didn't have an answer. But Zack, walking just ahead,

turned and met my eyes. "We've come this far," he said. "We *have* to see this through."

Jayden adjusted his glasses, eyes narrowed in thought. "Maybe the answers are at the summit. If this was created for a reason, someone—*something*—must know why."

A chill ran down my spine, but I nodded. "Then let's go."

The path wound higher and higher, until the ground beneath us flattened into a wide plateau. In the center, a massive stone archway stood, covered in glowing carvings that looked like the ones we had seen in the cave. The moment we stepped closer, the air changed.

It *felt* ancient.

Time itself seemed to slow, and then... *it appeared*.

A shimmering figure emerged from an archway, its form shifting like mist, but its eyes—deep, glowing pools of green—locked onto us with an intensity that sent a shiver down my spine.

The shimmering figure of the ancient being wavered, like mist curling in the wind. But then—just as I was preparing for some grand, mystical explanation—it solidified into something *completely* unexpected.

The boy from the bridge.

With the same cocky grin, same messy hair, and same ridiculous sense of humor.

"*Oh man!* You should have seen your faces!" he said, laughing and doubling over as if he had just pulled the best prank in the history of time. "Priceless. Absolutely priceless."

I blinked, trying to process what was happening. "*You?!*" I sputtered. "You're the ancient being?!"

Zack groaned, rubbing his temples. "Of *course* it's you. Why am I not even surprised?"

Jayden, for once, was completely speechless. Sofia, however, crossed her arms and glared. "Are you kidding me? You've been messing with us this whole time?!"

The boy—guardian, spirit, *whatever* he was—grinned wider. "Messing with you? Nah, I'd call it... observing. Guiding. *Entertaining myself while you ran around like lost hatchlings.*" He stretched his arms above his head like he'd just woken up from a nap. "And boy, have you all been *fun* to watch."

My fists clenched. "We almost *died* a dozen times."

He shrugged. "Yeah, well, that's part of the test. And you passed, so congrats." He gave us two thumbs up. "A+ adventurers."

I was so ready to throw a light javelin at him.

Zack let out a frustrated sigh. "Alright, fine. You win. But *who are you really*? And why are you here?"

The boy smirked, then leaned against the massive stone archway like he had all the time in the world. "Alright, alright. I *guess* I owe you some answers. First off, name's Elias—not 'random bridge kid,' though I *kinda* liked that one." He winked at me, and I glared harder. "Second, I've been here a *long* time. Like, 'longer-than-your-entire-history-class' long. And third…" His grin softened, and for the first time, he looked serious. "This island isn't just a test. It's a *prison*."

Silence.

The wind howled through the mountains, whipping at our clothes, but none of us spoke.

Finally, Jayden swallowed. "A prison? For *what*?"

Elias leaned back, looking up at the sky as if choosing his words carefully. "For power," he said. "For knowledge. For things that *shouldn't* be out there in the real world." He gestured vaguely at the mountain beneath us. "This place? It was built to contain the Elemental Stone. Not to protect it. Not to use it. But to *lock it away*."

I felt my breath hitch. "But… why? It doesn't feel evil."

Elias tilted his head, his expression unreadable. "Because power *by itself* isn't evil," he admitted. "But what people *do* with it?" His eyes darkened. "That's a different story."

I looked down at the stone in my hand. It pulsed faintly, warm and alive, like it had a heartbeat of its own. The thought of *not* returning it to its rightful place made my stomach twist.

"But if it was locked away," Sofia said, "why let *us* find it?"

Elias raised a brow. "Well, that's the big question, isn't it?" He stepped closer, tapping the stone lightly with a finger. "The truth is… the island chose you."

Zack scoffed. "Great. Love being 'chosen' by an ancient island full of dinosaurs and death."

Elias laughed. "Yeah, well, you've done *better* than most." He crossed his arms, smirking. "You wanna know why you're *really* here?"

I nodded, gripping the Elemental Stone tighter.

His smile faded. "Because the island is dying. And without that stone in its rightful place..." He sighed. "Everything will collapse. The creatures, the magic, even this whole floating chunk of land? *Gone.*"

My stomach twisted. We had fought so hard, survived so much—*but* we had also made things worse by taking the stone.

"And what happens to *us* if we return it?" Jayden asked, his voice unusually quiet.

Elias tilted his head. "Ah. That's the real kicker, isn't it?" He glanced between us, then gave a lopsided grin. "Honestly? No idea."

Sofia's jaw dropped. "Are you *serious*?!"

"Hey, I've never *seen* someone return it," Elias said, holding up his hands in mock surrender. "So I can't tell you what happens. Maybe you get to go home. Maybe you get superpowers. Maybe you *become* part of the island." His grin widened. "Guess there's only one way to find out."

Zack shook his head, muttering, "This is *so* unfair."

I exhaled, my fingers tightening around the stone. I wanted to be angry, to demand better answers, but deep down… I knew there weren't any. This was the truth. The island was dying. We had taken something we weren't meant to have.

And now, we had to fix it.

I turned to my friends, meeting each of their eyes. Jayden's face was full of quiet understanding. Sofia looked conflicted but determined. And Zack—frustrated, stubborn Zack—sighed and ran a hand through his hair.

"Well," he muttered, "we've come this far."

I nodded. "Then let's finish this."

Elias grinned, stepping aside and motioning toward the summit. "That's the spirit. But be warned—now that you're close, the island's *real* protectors aren't gonna let you waltz up there without a fight."

Zack groaned. "Of course not."

I squared my shoulders, feeling the familiar hum of power in my bracelet. "Then I guess they'll have to *try* and stop us."

Elias let out a low whistle. "Oh, I *like* you."

We moved forward, past him and toward the final climb.

Behind us, Elias chuckled. "Good luck. You're *definitely* gonna need it."

CHAPTER 17
ZACK – THE SUMMIT

The summit loomed ahead, a jagged peak of white stone wrapped in swirling mist. My breath came in short bursts, not from exhaustion—I was used to the climb by now—but from the weight pressing down on my chest. This was it. The end of the journey.

And yet, it didn't *feel* like an ending.

More like a moment teetering on the edge of something bigger.

I gritted my teeth and pushed forward, my boots crunching against frost-covered rock. Charles padded along beside me, his fiery-red scales glowing faintly in the thin mountain air. Every so often, he let out a soft growl, his sharp eyes flicking around the path like he was expecting trouble.

He wasn't the only one.

Jayden was quiet, one hand resting lightly on Charles'

back. He was thinking, calculating—his mind always working two steps ahead. Sofia, on the other hand, was gripping her sword so tightly her knuckles had gone white. Her usual sarcasm had faded into silent focus. Addy was just ahead of me, her light-orbs hovering around her like tiny guardian stars. She was tense, her shoulders squared, but I could see the way her eyes flicked to me every few steps. Checking on me.

I met her gaze and gave a small nod. *I'm okay.*

She nodded back. *Good.*

The summit leveled out into a massive plateau, smooth stone stretching out beneath a sky full of swirling clouds. At the very center, a circular platform rose from the ground, carved with glowing symbols that pulsed in time with the stone in Addy's hands. A pedestal stood in the middle of it all, waiting.

Waiting for *us*.

"We made it," Jayden said, his voice filled with quiet awe.

But we weren't celebrating yet.

Sofia shifted uncomfortably. "Yeah. A little *too* easy, don't you think?"

"Way too easy," I muttered.

We had spent *days* fighting our way through this island. Every step of the journey had been a test. A challenge. Why would this final moment be any different?

"It's a trap," Addy said, stepping closer to the pedestal. "It *has* to be."

Elias' words echoed in my head. *Now that you're close, the island's real protectors aren't gonna let you waltz up there without a fight.*

I swallowed hard. "We're not alone."

Charles suddenly snapped to attention, his head lifting, eyes locked on the swirling mist beyond the platform. A low, rumbling growl built in his throat.

Jayden's fingers twitched toward his bracelet. "Something's coming."

Then, as if responding to his words, the mist *moved.*

Shapes slithered and flickered in the haze—shadows with glowing eyes, bodies shifting like smoke and fire. The air vibrated with a low hum, like the mountain itself was waking up. The stone beneath our feet cracked, energy sparking up from the glowing symbols, and suddenly—

They stepped forward.

Tall figures, wreathed in mist and light, armor gleaming like polished moonstone. They looked human, but their eyes—bright and burning with raw energy— held something *ancient.* Something *inhuman.*

The island's *real* guardians.

One of them stepped forward, their voice like rolling thunder.

"You do not belong here."

The words rippled through the air, heavy with power. My hands clenched into fists.

"We didn't come to steal anything," Addy said, standing firm. "We're *returning* the stone."

The guardian tilted their head, as if considering her words. Then they lifted their hand, and the air *shifted*—a pressure like an unseen weight pressing down on my chest.

"Then prove you are worthy."

The moment the words left their mouth, the air *exploded*.

Lightning struck the platform, sending a shockwave of energy crashing into us. I threw up my arms, barely holding my ground as the wind howled around us.

"*Here we go!*" I shouted, drawing my sword.

The guardians *moved*—fast, like shifting shadows, their forms flickering between solid and mist as they rushed toward us.

Charles let out a deafening screech and leapt forward, flames bursting from his mouth as he slashed at one of the figures. The guardian barely flinched, deflecting the attack with a glowing blade of their own.

Jayden threw out his hands, his magic surging through Charles, amplifying his fire into an inferno. Sofia met one of the guardians head-on, her sword flashing in the storm-lit air as she clashed against their glowing weapon.

I didn't have time to watch.

One of them was coming *for me*.

I barely had a second to react before a blade of pure light came swinging toward my head. I ducked, rolling across the stone as I summoned a spear from my bracelet. It pulsed with the enchantment I had given it—*Elemental*

Boon—and as I lunged forward, the blade crackled with power.

The guardian blocked it effortlessly, but I wasn't done.

I twisted, using my momentum to bring my boot up in a sharp kick. It *connected*, sending the guardian stumbling back just enough for me to regroup.

"Zack!" Addy called, throwing a javelin of light at the figure in front of me. They dodged, but I used the distraction to press forward, slashing my sword toward their chest.

This time, they didn't block fast enough.

The blade sliced through their form, and for a split second, the mist flickered, revealing something *real* beneath the shifting energy.

I hesitated.

And that's when they struck.

A blast of energy hit me square in the chest, sending me skidding backward across the stone. I barely caught myself before going over the edge.

"Not—*cool*," I coughed, pushing myself to my feet.

Addy was already moving, sending waves of magic in every direction, covering Sofia as she fought. Jayden had his hands on Charles, focusing all his energy into the raptor's flames.

And me?

I was *done* playing defense.

Gritting my teeth, I reached for my magic—not just

the crafting, but something *deeper*. Something I had felt ever since I enchanted my armor.

The island's magic.

The power surged through me, rushing into my sword, my armor, my very *breath*. I *felt* the connection—between the stone, the island, and even these guardians.

They weren't just testing us.

They were *waiting* for us to understand.

I lifted my sword and pointed it at the lead guardian.

"We're not your enemies," I said. "We're not here to destroy. We're here to *restore*."

The guardian studied me, their glowing eyes unreadable. The others hesitated, their movements slowing.

Addy stepped beside me. "Let us finish this."

The energy in the air *shifted*.

The storm above settled. The mist began to fade.

And then—

The guardian lowered their blade.

"You may proceed."

The battle was over.

But the final challenge still awaited.

CHAPTER 18
ADDY – THE LAST STAND

The moment my foot touched the pedestal, the ground shook.

Not the small tremors we'd felt before. Not the slow, eerie shift of the island reacting to our presence.

This was something else.

Something *angry*.

The Elemental Stone pulsed in my hands, the swirling energy inside it flashing between colors, wild and chaotic. I tightened my grip, glancing at the others. Zack was already moving closer, his sword drawn, his jaw set. Jayden put a steadying hand on Charles' back, his raptor letting out a low growl, sensing the shift in the air. Sofia adjusted her grip on her sword, her fingers twitching at her inventory bracelet like she was ready to pull out *everything* if it came down to it.

Then, from the shadows beyond the summit—they came.

Massive creatures, slinking forward like nightmares pulled from every danger we had faced so far.

A gargantuan centipede, its shell gleaming like polished stone, *clicking* its venomous fangs as it rose up on dozens of legs. A serpent with glistening, black scales and too many eyes, its forked tongue flicking out as it *tasted* the magic in the air. A winged beast, its shape shifting between bird and bat, its crimson eyes locking onto us as it let out a scream that made my bones vibrate.

This wasn't just a test.

This was the island's last defense.

The final challenge before we could restore the Elemental Stone.

The Last Stand.

Zack was the first to react, charging forward without hesitation, his copper armor flaring with the enchantment he had placed on it. His sword clashed against the armored legs of the centipede, sparks flying as his blade barely scratched its exoskeleton.

"Jayden, control that snake!" I called, moving toward the pedestal.

Jayden focused, extending his hands toward the writhing serpent. His bondsmith abilities flared, his magic reaching out—*grasping* for control.

The snake shuddered—hesitated—but then its many eyes locked on Jayden and it struck.

Charles leapt in front of Jayden, flames erupting from his mouth, forcing the serpent back.

Sofia didn't wait for orders. She was already moving, a blur as she dodged past Zack and leapt at the winged creature, her sword flashing in the dimming light.

I ran.

Straight for the pedestal.

The Elemental Stone was singing in my hands, thrumming with power as if it knew this was the moment it was meant for.

I barely made it three steps before the centipede swung at me.

I dove, rolling to the side as its massive tail slammed into the stone, sending cracks splitting outward.

Zack slammed his shoulder into its body, trying to force it back. "Go!" he shouted at me.

I tried.

I really tried.

I pushed forward, raising a hard-light shield as the winged beast dived for me. Its talons raked against the barrier, the force nearly knocking me off my feet.

I dug my heels in and fought back.

"Not today," I hissed, launching a spear of pure light at the creature. It dodged, but I didn't have time to keep up the fight.

I turned toward the pedestal—just in time to see the centipede whip its massive tail toward Zack.

"ZACK!" I screamed.

He turned, raising his sword too late.

But Charles was faster.

The raptor leapt, his flaming body slamming into the centipede's tail, sending a wave of fire scorching across the summit. The centipede screeched, its shell glowing red-hot where Charles had hit it.

Zack rolled away, coming up beside me, breathing hard.

"We need to end this," he panted.

"I know," I said, gripping the Elemental Stone.

We met eyes.

And in that moment, we both knew exactly what we needed to do.

"Cover me," I said.

Zack nodded. No hesitation.

I turned back toward the pedestal and ran.

Jayden and Charles worked together, driving the serpent back. Sofia dodged and weaved, her sword flashing as she kept the winged beast occupied.

And Zack—Zack stood at my back.

Every time one of the creatures tried to stop me, he was there.

His enchanted sword clashed against the centipede's fangs. His traps, hastily crafted, snapped shut on its legs, slowing it down.

The winged beast dove, but Sofia shouted —"Duck!"—and I dropped just in time for her sword to slice through its wing.

We were doing it.

We were winning.

And then—I was there.

At the pedestal.

I raised the Elemental Stone.

It pulsed, the colors within shifting faster, brighter, filling my hands with heat.

And then—

I placed it where it belonged.

The moment the stone touched the pedestal, everything changed.

A pulse of energy blasted outward, sending the creatures reeling.

The centipede shrieked, its body shattering into dust.

The serpent hissed, its many eyes closing as it slithered away into the mist.

The winged beast, bleeding, gave a final, mournful cry before fading into shadows.

And then—silence.

The sky, which had been raging with storm clouds, stilled.

The wind died down.

And the Elemental Stone...glowed.

The pedestal absorbed its light, the carvings flaring with energy, spreading outward across the mountain.

I stumbled back, Zack catching me before I fell.

It was done.

The Last Stand...was over.

And now...we would see what happened next.

CHAPTER 19
ZACK – THE RETURN OF THE STONE

The moment the Elemental Stone settled into place, **the world shifted**.

Light exploded outward, not just from the pedestal, but from the entire **mountain**. It **raced** down the stone, following cracks that weren't there before, carving glowing veins into the rock as if the very earth was **coming alive**.

The storm clouds above **swirled**, parting like curtains to reveal a sky that was no longer just sky—but a swirling, **impossible mix** of colors, shifting between deep blues, fiery oranges, and streaks of gold that crackled like lightning.

I staggered back, my body **buzzing** with energy. It was **everywhere**—pulsing in the air, thrumming through my bones, vibrating through the copper armor I'd crafted.

And then, all at once, the **island responded**.

The jungle below **shimmered**, trees growing **taller**, vibrant green leaves unfurling like they had been waiting for this moment to **breathe** again. The rivers that wound through the land **glowed** with streaks of blue, the water **rushing faster**, purer, as if the land was waking up from a long **sleep**.

The Elemental Stone had **never** just been a simple treasure.

It was the **heart of the island.**

And we had just set it **free.**

A sudden, deep **rumbling** shook the summit beneath my feet, and I turned to Addy, heart hammering. "Tell me that's supposed to happen."

She stared at the stone, her hands clenched into fists. "I don't know," she admitted. "But I think it's too late to stop it."

I swallowed, looking out over the **changing** island.

Then something else caught my eye.

A point of **light**, forming above the pedestal.

No—not just **light**.

A **tear in reality.**

The air **ripped open**, colors bending around it like a wound in the sky, and through it, I saw—

Home.

Not some magical paradise, not another challenge waiting for us.

I saw the **hallway of our school.**

I saw the rows of lockers, the linoleum floor, the faint flicker of a broken fluorescent light buzzing overhead.

It was like **no time had passed**.

Like we had **never left.**

"Guys," I breathed. "That's it. That's our way back."

Jayden stepped beside me, **staring** at the portal, his hand resting on Charles' back. The raptor let out a low, uneasy growl, but Jayden only whispered something to calm him.

Sofia moved closer, her face unreadable, her eyes darting between the portal and the island.

And Addy—

She was looking at me.

Like she was waiting for me to **say something**.

For me to **decide**.

I looked back at the **island**, at everything we had survived. The jungle, the swamp, the mountain. The creatures that had tested us, the people—well, **ghosts**—we had met, the powers we had **discovered**.

We had **changed** here.

We weren't the same kids who had walked into that classroom expecting just another boring day.

We were **more**.

And now...we had to leave.

I turned to my friends, my team—**my family**.

"We did it," I said, my voice **steady**, even as my heart twisted. "We're going home."

Addy gave me a small, almost **sad** smile. "Yeah," she whispered. "I guess we are."

I took a deep breath, then looked down at Ash, my mechanical bird perched on my shoulder.

"We can bring them, right?" I asked, feeling a strange **fear** rise in my chest. "We won't have to leave them?"

Ash **chirped**, tilting his head.

Jayden frowned. "I don't know..." He hesitated, looking at Charles, then at the portal. "We should try."

Sofia stepped forward first, holding out her hand, her snake coiling tight around her wrist. "Then let's find out."

I watched as she **stepped through**.

For a moment, she **flickered**, like she was being stretched between worlds.

Then she was **gone**.

A heavy silence fell over us.

I clenched my fists. "Okay. Guess that means it works."

Jayden let out a shaky breath. "I guess we'll find out if the companions can come through too."

He gave Charles one last look, then whispered something in his ear.

Then he stepped into the portal, Charles **right beside him**.

Another flicker.

Another moment of breathless silence.

Then they were **gone** too.

I turned to Addy, and for the first time, I saw hesitation in her eyes.

"We'll be okay," I promised.

She nodded, then, before I could say anything else, she **stepped forward**.

She vanished.

I was alone.

I let out a breath, then looked back at the **island** one last time.

We had **won**.

We had **survived**.

And now...it was **time**.

I stepped forward.

The portal **pulled me in**.

And in the blink of an eye—

The island was **gone**.

CHAPTER 20
ADDY – HOMECOMING

The first thing I noticed was the silence.

No wind. No jungle sounds. No roar of distant dinosaurs or the rustling of leaves from something unseen.

Just the hum of old fluorescent lights.

I blinked. My hands were gripping the straps of my backpack, and I was sitting in the same desk I had been in when this all started. The classroom was exactly the same —the posters on the wall, the rows of empty chairs, the faint smell of dry erase markers and stale air.

Detention.

Like nothing had ever happened.

Except—I knew it had.

I turned to Zack, who was staring at his hands like he half-expected them to glow. Jayden was adjusting his glasses with shaky fingers, and Sofia was just frozen, her expression unreadable.

We were all back.

But Mr. Shadow was gone.

His desk sat empty, not even a single paper left behind. The whiteboard was blank. The clock above the door ticked forward like this was just any other day.

I swallowed, my heart pounding.

Had it been real? The dinosaurs, the Elemental Stone, the magic? The fight on the mountain, the friendships, the adventures?

Then my fingers brushed against something cold on my wrist.

I looked down—and my breath hitched.

It was a bracelet. A golden charm bracelet.

Hanging from it was a tiny, intricately detailed monkey—Cappy, my little mechanical companion. The moment I touched it, warmth spread through my chest, and I could feel him, like a distant presence in the back of my mind.

I looked up at the others, my heart racing.

Zack had one too—his had a tiny metal bird. Ash.

Jayden had two. One was a fox, the other a raptor. He blinked at them, then closed his eyes for a second.

When he opened them, he whispered, "I can still feel Charles."

Sofia turned her wrist, staring at a tiny silver snake, a mix of awe and something sad flickering across her face.

We hadn't just imagined it.

The island was real.

And somehow—some way—we were still connected to it.

The door to the classroom creaked open.

A different teacher stood in the doorway, her arms crossed. "Detention is over," she said, like we hadn't just vanished to another world and saved an entire island.

We all exchanged one last look, a silent conversation passing between us.

We had changed.

We weren't just the same four kids who had walked into this room earlier. We were something more now. Stronger. Wiser. A team.

And even though we were home, we weren't saying goodbye.

Because deep down, in the quiet spaces of our minds—

The island was still calling.

And one day, we might just answer.

The End.

(For now.)

LEAVE A REVIEW

Thank you for reading. Please leave a review.

Check out my website at AuthorTimothyMcGowen.com

If you really liked the book, please consider reaching out and telling me what you enjoyed about it at, Timothy. mcgowen1@gmail.com.

Join my Facebook group and discuss the books at: https://www.facebook.com/groups/234653175151521/

Join my Patreon at: https://www.patreon.com/TimothyMcGowen

ABOUT THE AUTHOR

Timothy McGowen was born in Modesto, California. His journey into stories started with reading the Goosebumps books. Later he read a novel by Terry Brooks and became hooked on fantasy/scifi almost instantly. Shortly after that he was given a school assignment to write a 5 page fiction story, and 25 pages later his story was half done. He hasn't stopped writing since.

His popular Arcane Knight series has sold thousands of copies in both ebook and audible so far. Consider signing up for my newsletter for news on book releases as they become available.

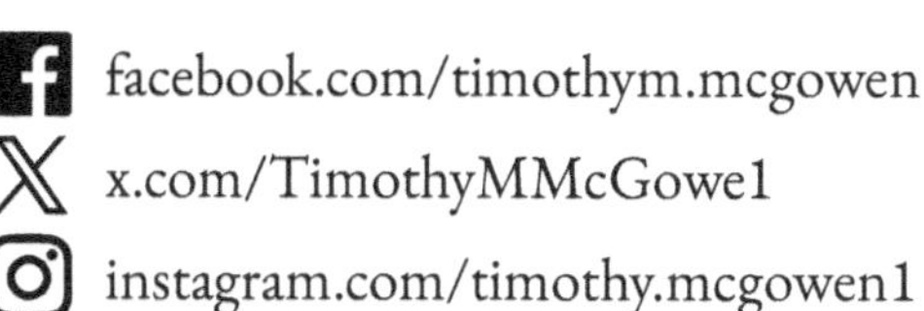

facebook.com/timothym.mcgowen

x.com/TimothyMMcGowe1

instagram.com/timothy.mcgowen1

LITRPG GROUP

Check out this group if you want to gather together and hear about new great LitRPG books.

(https://www.facebook.com/groups/LitRPGGroup/)

LEARN MORE ABOUT LITRPG/GAMELIT GENRE

To learn more about LitRPG & GameLit, talk to author and just have an awesome time by joining some LitRPG/Gamelit groups.

Here is another LitRPG group you can join if you are looking for the next great read!

Facebook.com/groups/LitRPG.books

List of LitRPG/Gamelit Facebook Groups:

- https://www.facebook.com/groups/ LitRPGReleases/
- https://www.facebook.com/groups/ litrpgforum/
- https://www.facebook.com/groups/ litrpglegends/
- https://www.facebook.com/groups/ LitRPGsociety/
- https://www.facebook.com/groups/ AleronKong/